MURDER SO DEEP

Eagle Cove Mysteries #1

NORA CHASE
ANNE CHASE

Thomas Publishing

To the writing gang at Crossroads —
for inspiring me to explore my love of mysteries

CHAPTER 1

I gripped the sledgehammer tightly, the wooden handle smooth to the touch, and weighed the consequences of my intended act. There would be dust, yes. Broken pieces of brick, certainly. A mess to be cleaned up, without question.

But at least I would know. With so many decisions resting on my shoulders, there was value in clarity. Especially when it came to what Jerry Meachum was proposing.

Because either Jerry was a good, competent, trustworthy plumber.

Or not.

Hair fell across my cheek, and with an irritated sigh I pushed it back. Minutes earlier, upstairs in the light of day, my shiny new idea had been just that — a shiny new idea — and I'd been filled with resolve. But now, here in the basement, sledgehammer in hand, doubt was creeping in.

The wall appeared a bit rough, yes, and perhaps a bit discolored. The bricks and mortar were uneven. But nothing was damp to the touch, and nothing smelled of mold or rot. If Jerry was right — if the pipe behind the wall was leaking — then wouldn't there be evidence of that? Wouldn't something be wet? Wouldn't something stink?

You're being silly, Sarah. Go back upstairs. There were a million things I could be doing instead of contemplating violence in the basement of my great-aunt's building. Gazing at the dusty bricks, I found myself shaking my head. For over a century, these humble blocks of heated clay had done their job without complaint. They'd stood their ground and kept the building on solid footing.

Who was I to bash them in?

And yet....

A growl escaped my lips.

I had to know.

Before another sliver of doubt could sneak in, I raised the sledgehammer and swung hard. The sharp crack of metal on brick ricocheted through the room. I swung again, then again. A cloud of dust billowed forth as brick and mortar crumbled.

Blinking and coughing, I stepped back. I'd always been comfortable engaging in physical tasks that men considered their exclusive domain; in a different life, I might have renovated homes for a living. The overhead light, a single bare bulb, shone brightly enough to reveal a hole where a half-dozen bricks had stood just seconds before. The hole was bigger than I'd expected — big enough for a bowling ball to fit through, and to see into the empty space inside.

Swinging the hammer had felt good. I felt refreshed, even exhilarated, as the tension and stress of the past week momentarily receded.

After setting down the sledgehammer, I peered into the hole. Too dark. I sniffed. There was a smell of *something*, but what? I'd need a flashlight.

I made my way up, the old wooden stairs creaking with every step. When I reached the hallway on the ground floor, I heard a throat being cleared and a voice say, "Sarah, what in the world are you doing?"

The voice, raspy and querulous, belonged to Mr. Benson, one of my great-aunt's tenants, who was peering down at me from the second-floor landing. He was a dapper fellow in his seventies, dressed in a tweed jacket and red bow tie. His bony hand gripped the railing.

Another voice joined his. "Stop that racket, you old crank!"

"Old?" Mr. Benson said, shifting his attention to the new voice. "*Me*? Pot calling kettle, woman!"

Gabby McBride, the second floor's other tenant,

joined Mr. Benson at the railing. Her soft white hair and daffodil print dress, a swirl of yellow and Easter blue, suggested — wrongly — that she was sweetness and light.

Gabby transferred her scowl from Mr. Benson to me. "Sarah, was that you banging?"

"Yes," I said. "Sorry. I'm checking the pipes for leaks."

"Checking the pipes?" Mr. Benson said with a frown. "Where?"

"In the basement."

"Young lady, why would you do that?"

"To visually inspect the pipes."

He shot a glance at Gabby. "Basement, you said? Which wall?"

"The brick wall near the furnace."

"*You silly girl!*" Gabby yelled. "What's gotten into you?" She raced down the stairs, her cane swinging wildly in front of her, her feet a blur.

Startled by the speed of her descent, I retreated a step. "Jerry Meachum said the low water pressure — which you complained about just yesterday? — could be due to leaky pipes."

"Jerry Meachum?" Gabby snorted, gazing up at me in disbelief. She was a tiny woman, barely clearing five feet, but she knew how to intimidate. "That boy is a *moron*. Surely you remember that?"

I did remember — even as a kid, Jerry had been slow on the uptake — but that didn't mean he hadn't learned enough to be decent at his job. I opened my mouth but realized, just in time, that I couldn't hope to win this argument. Instead I said, "It's a small hole, and I already made it, so there's nothing more to worry about."

"Now, young lady," Mr. Benson said, also making his way down the stairs, but carefully. "I know your great-aunt left you in charge, but there's no need for any of this."

"If there's a leak, I need to know," I said. "So do prospective buyers."

"I'm sure everything's fine," Mr. Benson continued.

"I have a flashlight up front," I said. "Back in a second."

Despite their protests, I dashed to the building's front room — once a cafe, now a dusty storeroom — and rummaged through my handbag until my fingers closed over my trusty light.

"Found it," I said to them, holding it up as I returned to the hallway.

"My dear, there's no need," Mr. Benson repeated.

"For once, the old crank is right," Gabby added.

"This won't take but a minute," I replied.

I slipped past them, flashlight in hand, and made my way down the stairs. Still protesting noisily, the two of them followed, the wooden steps groaning ominously under the added weight.

The overhead bulb cast enough light to clearly illuminate the hole I'd smashed in. I stepped over the broken bricks, clicked on the flashlight, and aimed the beam inside.

The space behind the wall was deeper than I'd expected — nearly two feet. Moving the beam to the left, I found the pipe that Jerry speculated might be the leaker. Starting at the top of the pipe, I slowly ran the light down it, checking for signs of damage.

Behind me, Gabby and Mr. Benson had gone quiet. Which seemed — odd. I turned to find them staring at me, side by side, still as statues.

"See?" I gave them a reassuring smile. "Nothing to worry about."

I resumed my inspection, following the pipe downward.

On the floor next to the pipe, the light landed on a large bundle of some sort. Bulky. Wrapped in clear plastic.

Frowning, I tried to process what I was seeing.

Then I gasped, a shock of horror jolting through me.

Inside the clear plastic, the bundle had a wrist — and the wrist was wearing a man's watch!

CHAPTER 2

The sheriff's deputy pointed me to a chair and table near the front window. "Please have a seat, ma'am."

I sat down and glanced toward the back of the room, where Gabby and Mr. Benson were being interviewed by another deputy. Late-afternoon sun filtered through the big storefront window, casting long shadows over a space that, a decade ago, had been home to a thriving cafe but now was used for storage. The air smelled musty and stale. The furnishings — the booths, the tables and chairs, the display counters once filled with pies and muffins and cookies — were still here, covered in drop cloths, a sad reminder of what once was.

The deputy slipped in opposite me, pen and notepad in hand, gazing at me with the awkwardness of an earnest puppy. He seemed so *young* — like puberty hadn't finished with him. Did he even shave? Was that peach fuzz on his cheeks? His uniform appeared a couple of sizes too large for his thin frame.

"You need anything, ma'am? A glass of water?"

"I'm fine, thanks." At least Deputy Peach Fuzz was polite. I wondered idly if I knew his parents. "So how do we do this?"

He cleared his throat. "I'm supposed to collect basic information for the sheriff."

"Fire away."

He furrowed his brow, unsure if I was trying to joke with him. "You called it in?"

"That's right."

"About thirty minutes ago?"

"That's right."

I wondered if I would ever be able to erase from my mind the image of the man's watch beneath the clear plastic — and beneath the watch, the dried-out, leathery skin of *the dead man's hand*....

"Your full name, ma'am?"

"Sarah Boone."

"Age?"

"Forty-two."

"Address?"

I gave him my address in California. He looked up from his scribbling, puzzled.

"I'm visiting," I said. "Staying at my mother's."

"And your mother is?"

"Nancy Boone."

"Oh, I've met her. Works for the mayor?"

"Yes. She's the office manager."

He breathed in. "That means you're the grand-niece."

"Yes, my great-aunt Emily is — was — the owner of this building."

Sympathy played across his face. "I met your aunt when she ran the Harvest Festival. She was a great lady. I'm sorry about what happened. My condolences for your loss."

Tears snuck up on me, but I managed to push them back. Now was *not* the time for emotion. Over the past week, I'd had more than my fill.

I decided it was time to stop holding this young man's age against him. "What's your name, Deputy?"

"Wilkerson, ma'am."

I stuck out my hand. "Pleased to meet you, Deputy Wilkerson."

He hesitated, as if unsure what to do, then put out his hand. "Thank you, ma'am." He had a nice face, open and boyish, and short-cropped brown hair.

"You can call me Sarah."

He gave me an earnest smile. "When I'm off-duty, sure."

"Got it. So right now, you need to keep it official."

Another smile. "Totally. I mean, yes, ma'am."

"Tell me what you need to know."

He paused, then said, "I heard she left the building to you."

"My great-aunt? Yes, that's right."

"And I hear you're selling it?"

"That's right."

"Sorry," he said. "It's just … small town and all, you hear things."

"Oh, I know. I used to live here."

"You lived in Eagle Cove? When?"

Before you were even born, I almost said. "I was raised here, then left for college in Boston. After college, I got married and moved to California."

He asked about the day's events, and I took him through what had happened.

As he scribbled in his notebook, it began to sink in that what had happened was indeed note*worthy*. After the shock of discovery, I'd gone back into the hole in the basement wall, running my light slowly over what I'd found. The body was fully encased in a clear plastic shower curtain. Though it was difficult to tell for sure, the body appeared to be wearing pants, a dark jacket, and dark shoes. From my angle, I couldn't get a good view of the head. The only skin I could see was the wrist and part of the hand. The faint smell I'd noticed earlier was more noticeable now — unpleasant and sharp, but hardly the stench of death I expected. The skin's leathery texture suggested the body had been dried out, perhaps even mummified.

The rush of questions flooding through me had been interrupted by Gabby and Mr. Benson, who had abandoned silence and were noisily demanding a look themselves. Reluctantly, after warning them not to touch anything, I'd handed them the flashlight and raced upstairs to call 911. When I'd returned to the basement, I'd found them whispering angrily. Then the deputies had arrived, escorted us upstairs, and asked us to wait in the cafe for the sheriff.

Deputy Wilkerson's phone buzzed. He read a message on it and stood up. "Sheriff and the coroner are on the way."

"Anything else you need from me?" I asked.

He shut his notepad. "I'm good for now."

"You want me to wait here for the sheriff?"

"Yes, ma'am. If you don't mind."

"I'm fine. Go do what you need to do."

He gave me a grateful smile and headed out, presumably to make sure the basement was ready for the sheriff's arrival.

In the back of the room, Gabby and Mr. Benson were in a booth with a second deputy. Earlier, I'd overheard bits and pieces of Mr. Benson's account of what happened, his voice carrying across the room.

Now apparently it was Gabby's turn. In a

quavering voice so soft I could barely hear her, she said, "Oh, my, yes, Deputy — such a shock."

I breathed in with surprise. Gabby sounded so *helpless*. So overwhelmed, bewildered, frail....

"Please take your time, Ms. McBride," the deputy said. "No need to rush."

"Thank you, dear," Gabby whispered. "You're so kind. I try my best, but sometimes, it's hard to keep things clear...."

I bit my lip and willed myself to keep my expression neutral.

What.

A.

Crock.

"I just can't believe," Gabby continued, adding a fluttery uncertainty to her performance, as if lacking the strength to even finish her sentence, "that something like this could happen here, in the very place I live...."

The deputy, a young woman not much older than Deputy Wilkerson, nodded sympathetically. Her black hair was pulled back into a bun. She seemed concerned about Gabby's condition, but something about the set of her shoulders suggested caution, like she was reserving judgment. "Mr. Benson has given us enough for now, Ms. McBride. Would you like me to help you upstairs to your apartment?"

"Oh, you are so sweet," Gabby said. "Perhaps

in a bit? Best I sit still for a moment and gather my energy...."

"Can I get you something? A glass of water?"

"A cup of tea?" Gabby said immediately. "With milk and two spoonfuls of sugar?"

The deputy blinked. "Tea? I'm not sure this place is set up...."

"It's not," I said, loudly enough for them to hear. I got to my feet and headed over. "But Mario's has some."

The deputy peered through the front window. "The restaurant across the street?"

"Best lasagna in town. I take it you're new to Eagle Cove?"

The deputy stood up. "Started with the department two weeks ago."

I extended my hand. "We haven't met. Sarah Boone."

"Deputy Martinez," the deputy said, returning the shake. "I'm not supposed to leave you."

"I'll stay with Ms. McBride," I said. "And I promise we won't touch a thing. Isn't that right, Mr. Benson?"

"Oh, yes," he said. "We'll stay right here, Deputy Martinez."

Before the deputy could suggest that I go for the tea instead of her, I added, "I bet your colleagues will want coffee, too. Ask for a big thermos. Mario's has a great dark roast and wonderful biscotti."

The deputy gave in. Though I couldn't be certain, I sensed she knew she'd been outmaneuvered. "I'll be right back. Mr. Benson, Ms. Boone, anything for you?"

I shook my head and so did Mr. Benson.

After a quick glance around the cafe, the deputy headed out the door and across the street.

Quickly, I slid into the booth opposite my great-aunt's two tenants.

They regarded me warily, still as statues.

"The sheriff's on his way and the deputies will be back any minute."

Mr. Benson cleared his throat. "My dear, I —"

"No, there's no time for that. You two need to come clean."

"My dear, what do you mean?"

"It's time to spill."

Across from me, two pairs of eyes widened.

Leaning closer, I said:

"What in the world is going on?"

CHAPTER 3

M r. Benson blinked first. He reared back in his seat, trying to act shocked and offended. "My dear," he spluttered. "If you think for one moment that I would have anything to do with … with … *murder*…."

"All I know," I said, "is what I saw and heard before the deputies arrived."

With a vibrant snort, Gabby roared to life. "What a load." Then she blasted me with the kind of fiery glare that makes kingdoms crumble and grown men cry.

Calmly, I hunkered down to repel the assault. My eyebrows were probably getting singed, but my spirit remained unbowed.

After a few seconds of heat and brimstone, I said, as sweetly yet firmly as I could, "You don't frighten me."

Mr. Benson let out a gasp.

Gabby ratcheted up her glare, still hoping to break through my defenses.

"Come on," I said, hoping to strike a reasonable tone. "Spill."

With a grunt of disgust, Gabby ceased her attack and switched tactics. "There's nothing to tell."

I shook my head. "You two knew."

She gave me a bewildered look. "Knew what?"

"You tried to stop me."

"Stop you from what? From making a mess and a racket? Of course we did, you silly girl. You were so loud! But if you're saying we knew that man was there…."

Mr. Benson cleared his throat. "Really, my dear, if you think…."

As I stared at the two of them, I found myself questioning what I'd seen and heard. Could I be wrong? Had I misinterpreted their angry whispered conversation in the basement, the one that ceased the moment I returned from calling the sheriff? Was their tense silence as we awaited the deputies simply a natural response to the shock of discovery? Was their eagerness to keep me from bashing a hole in the wall actually motivated by an innocent desire to prevent damage and avoid unnecessary noise? Was Gabby's frail act with the deputy the real deal?

No, I told myself. *These two are gigantic liars.*

"I'm not the enemy," I said.

"But you're not a friend," Gabby snapped. "Not anymore."

I blinked, surprised and stung. "What do you mean, not anymore?"

"You moved away decades ago. We don't know you anymore."

"If I'm not a friend," I said, trying to keep my voice neutral, "then what am I?"

"A stranger."

Hurt rushed in. A simple word — *stranger* — but it felt like a judgment.

Mr. Benson must have seen my disappointment. "Sarah," he said anxiously, "it's not that we don't like you. We *do* like you. What we're saying is that we need to get to know you again."

Before we can trust you, he didn't say.

Somehow, his words, spoken and not, made me feel worse.

"In the meantime," Gabby threw in, "keep your trap shut."

I nearly burst out laughing. *Bless you, too,* I almost said. But at least Gabby's rudeness had yanked me out of my moroseness.

And confirmed what I knew.

And not a moment too soon. I heard the sound of the building's hallway door open. A few seconds later, a man stepped into the cafe. He was grey-haired and in his mid-fifties, with a pinched, weathered face, dressed in slacks, button-down shirt, and blue windbreaker. His gaze traveled around the room before landing on us.

"Where's the body?" he said abruptly.

"Basement." I stood up. "The stairs are at the end of the hallway, on the right."

Without another word, he pivoted and left.

I glanced at Mr. Benson, who said, "Doc Barnes."

"Coroner?"

He shrugged. "Guess so. At least today? Maybe he helps out when needed? Normally he's our G.P."

"Not too friendly?"

"Hates people."

"Really?" I said, intrigued.

Before I could ask more, a second man stepped into the cafe.

And my world slowed to a standstill.

I should state here, for the record, that high school was a long time ago. A lot can change in a quarter-century. Since getting my diploma, I'd left Eagle Cove, attended college, gotten married, raised a daughter, and pushed my way through a divorce.

None of which I regretted, even the divorce. (Especially the divorce.) But in that moment, for a split second that seemed to expand, it was like the past twenty-five years had never happened. Suddenly I was back in high school again, sixteen years old again, a junior with a nerdy disposition and big glasses and the wrong hair and a fashion sense that could charitably be called a "mishmash." My stomach felt the same way it did that life-altering day when the new guy in school, the new senior everyone was talking about, walked up to me — me! — after chemistry class and introduced himself. Suddenly I was having trouble breathing, just like I had when the new senior — armed with his big wide smile, lively grey eyes, curly brown hair, and the power to draw me in like was he was a magnet and I was, I don't know, a bobby pin — stuck out his hand and said, "Hi, I'm Matt."

Our gazes locked. He blinked twice and went still. His cheeks flushed with emotion.

I resisted the impulse to run my hand through my hair, but my back and shoulders straightened involuntarily.

Time unfroze. He moved toward me. The intervening years had been kind to him — very kind. The high school boy had turned into a man. His face, once boyishly appealing, could now be accurately described as ruggedly handsome. His hair, still thick and curly, showed a few flecks of grey. His body, once lean and muscular, was now solid and muscular. He looked every inch the sheriff he apparently was.

Dear God, I thought. *I'm in trouble.*

"Sarah," he said as he reached me.

His physical proximity was, I was distressed to

discover, just as unsettling as it was all those years ago. He was still just as tall, his shoulders still just as broad, his attention still just as focused — as it had always seemed to be — on *me*.

I swallowed as I realized how foolishly I was behaving. A deer in headlights. A dumbstruck teenager. An idiot who couldn't let the past go.

Somehow I managed to say, "Matt, it's good to see you."

He didn't move, unable to keep his eyes off me. Then he blinked and his shoulders shifted and he took a step back. I could tell — when it came to him, I had always been able to tell — that his instinct was to pull me into his strong arms for a hug. But he didn't do that, maybe because he wasn't sure I wanted that. Or maybe because of the situation — him the sheriff, and me the witness who'd discovered a dead body....

I broke the tension by extending my hand. He followed my lead, his grip warm and firm. I felt a jolt at his touch.

"Good to see you, too, Sarah," he said, his voice low and rumbly. "You're looking great."

"Thank you," I said, my heart beating way too fast. I'd always liked the way he said my name. "You, too."

Our hands lingered.

He blinked again, then pulled away and swallowed. "I'm sorry about the circumstances."

"Yes, the circumstances," I repeated.

"I should go down to the basement and see…."

"Of course."

He started to leave, then turned back. "Listen," he said. "I'm truly very sorry about Emily."

The tears I'd been fighting earlier threatened to slip through. "Thank you."

"How are you and your mom holding up?"

"It's been a rough week."

He nodded sympathetically. "We'll talk later. But right now I've got to…."

"Of course. Go."

He left, my gaze following.

I took a deep breath, the shock of the moment rolling through me. Then I heard Gabby snort.

"What?" I said, suddenly rather angry at this rude woman.

Gabby was squinting at me, puzzled. "You didn't know, did you?"

I opened my mouth, but no words came out.

"Your mother didn't tell you he was the sheriff?"

I could only stare at her, flummoxed. Had Mom told me? It was entirely possible she had. She could talk up a storm when she got going, and I'd learned long ago — as a survival mechanism — to tune her out, lest I drown in the tsunami of words.

"He wasn't at the funeral," I said.

"He was out of town," she said. "Sheriff's business. Got home last night."

"How long has he been back in Eagle Cove?"

"Two years. Stepped in when old Sheriff Metzenberg retired."

I was about to ask more when I heard a throat being cleared. Deputy Wilkerson was at the doorway to the cafe.

"Ms. Boone, ma'am?" he said. "The sheriff and coroner want to see you in the basement."

CHAPTER 4

S till reeling from the shock of seeing my first boyfriend — *first love, first breakup, first regret, first everything* — after all these years, I followed Deputy Wilkerson to the basement.

The wooden stairs creaked as I made my way down. I'd never been a fan of basements, but now, knowing what lay behind the wall, I couldn't help but shiver.

Across the room, the coroner was peering into the hole. I heard him say, "Can't know till we run tests."

Matt watched me approach, his gaze somehow apologetic and professional at the same time. Even with only the single bare bulb providing illumination, I could see his regret and concern. "Sarah, sorry to have to bring you back down here."

"It's fine."

"We'd like you to take us through what happened."

"What do you want to know?" I said, relieved to hear myself sounding calm and composed.

"Whatever you can tell us. In your own words."

I took a breath, deciding where to begin. "Two days ago, I was doing a walk-through of the building and one of the tenants, Gabby McBride, said her water pressure was low, so I called Jerry Meachum. He came by yesterday and said there might be a leaky pipe behind the wall here. This afternoon I decided I didn't want to wait for Jerry to come back to find out, so I used that" — I pointed to the sledgehammer on the floor next to the broken bricks — "to knock a hole in the wall to see for myself."

Matt was giving me a look I knew all too well. *Some things never change*, he was thinking. But what he said was, "What happened then?"

"After I made the hole, I got a flashlight to check out the pipe and … found the body." With a shudder, I pushed back the memory of the dead man's leathery skin. "Then I went upstairs and called your office."

"I understand Gabby and Mr. Benson were with you as well."

"That's right. They heard me making the hole and came downstairs."

"Did they see the body?"

"Yes."

"After you did?"

"Yes."

"Did they remain downstairs when you went upstairs to call us?"

"Yes."

Matt said to the coroner, "Doc, any questions for Sarah?"

The coroner — who I needed to start thinking of as Doc Barnes — cleared his throat. "How long did your great-aunt own this building?"

I paused, thrown by the shift in topic. "She bought the building when she moved back to Eagle Cove. I was twelve. Which means … thirty years?"

"After she bought the building, she opened the cafe and moved into the apartment on the third floor."

"That's right."

"And took in tenants for the three apartments on the second floor."

"Yes."

"Including Donald Benson and Gabby McBride."

"That's right."

"When did they move in?"

"I'm not sure."

"And who were the other tenants?"

"Sorry, I don't know."

I found it interesting that it was the doc taking the lead. Maybe he liked being an investigator?

Or maybe Matt didn't want to be the one asking me official questions?

Doc Barnes continued. "Ten years ago, Emily closed the cafe."

"Yes, that's right."

"Why did she do that?"

I thought back, trying to recall. "She told me she got tired of running it."

"That's the reason she gave?"

"Yes." At the time, her decision had made sense to me — my great-aunt, then in her seventies, had been busy and active her entire life and deserved whatever kind of retirement she wanted for herself. "Are you suggesting there was another reason?"

Doc Barnes glanced at Matt, who cleared his throat and said, "We're just getting timelines down."

I gestured to the hole. "How long do you think the body's been there?"

"Can't tell at this point."

I frowned. "Surely you don't believe the body was placed there during the years my aunt owned and lived in the building?"

"Sarah…."

"You know my aunt. She would never be involved in anything like this."

"We're not saying she was."

"No," I said, "but you're keeping open the possibility."

He gave me a small smile. "Haven't changed, I see."

"Meaning?"

"I hope I don't have to ask you to not go digging."

"Digging? A deliberate word choice?"

"The department will get to the bottom of this, Sarah. I promise."

"So you *are* telling me to steer clear."

He let out a sigh. "Yes, I suppose I am."

His expressive grey eyes held a mixture of affection and firmness. Back in high school, he'd been more than happy to play along with my enthusiasms, whether it was traveling to Boston for a comic-book convention or spending a weekend traipsing through the woods counting birds for a school science project. But that was then and this was now. We weren't kids anymore. He was a law-enforcement professional and I was a witness to a crime.

I gave him a smile. "Okay, fine, I'll back off. But will you keep me informed of your progress?"

"Of course."

"What else do you need from me at this point?"

"We need you available for questions. Also, the basement is off-limits until we finish processing the scene."

I gestured to the hole in the wall. "When are you going to remove the body?"

"Tonight, I hope. We'll need to enlarge the hole and take brick and mortar for analysis."

"Of course."

"Is there anything else you can tell us?" he asked. "Anything that might be helpful?"

I paused, immediately leaping to Gabby and Mr. Benson's blazingly suspicious behavior. "No, nothing right now," I replied, trying to sound like I hadn't just decided to withhold potentially important evidence. "But if anything comes to mind...."

Matt's lips tightened, and I knew with a sinking feeling that he knew I was holding back. But before he could say anything, we heard an explosion of voices coming from above, followed by the loud clacking of heels on the wooden stairs.

"Sarah," my mother cried, rushing toward me and wrapping me in her arms. "Are you all right? I've been so worried!"

CHAPTER 5

My mother is a wonderful person and I love her dearly, but sometimes she drives me a bit batty.

It's an admission that always, without fail, makes me feel guilty.

Because when it comes to Mom, what's not to love? She's warm and energetic and expressive, with a big laugh and an even bigger heart. Most folks know her as Nancy Boone, the social dynamo with the sparkling green eyes and stylish auburn bob who knows everyone in town and lights up any room she's in. After Dad's death eight years ago, she took a job with the town of Eagle Cove and now works as office manager for the mayor, a role that perfectly aligns with her talents for organizing and socializing. She's a good listener (when she's not too busy talking) and always willing to pitch in and lend a helping hand. In short, she's a wonderful human being and most people are grateful to have her in their lives, including me.

No, the problem with my wonderful mom is that I'm not a wonderful daughter. That role in my family is played to perfection by my sister Grace, while mine is that of the daughter who doesn't call enough. I'm not a terrible daughter — really, truly, I'm not — but I know I can and should do better, especially in the communications department. Back when I was a teenager, I believed growing up was about breaking free. I also believed that, as I gained wisdom and maturity, I'd learn to better manage my responses to Mom's more exuberant impulses.

And yet, as her anxious maternal vise tightened, my first instinct was still to shrink away like a teenager embarrassed by the parental unit's public display of affection. Clearly, the acquisition of mother-related wisdom remained a work in progress.

To my credit, I managed to squelch any *actual* shrinking and instead said, "Mom, what are you doing here?"

"Are you okay, dear?" she asked, her hold tightening. "You must be in shock." I felt her shudder. "I can't even imagine."

"I'm fine," I said, beginning to plan my escape. "Really."

"Matthew," she said, her voice loud in my ear.

"Why did you have to drag Sarah back down to this awful basement?"

"Nancy —" Matt began.

"Don't you 'Nancy' me, young man. You should have taken Sarah's feelings into account before forcing her to come down here and relive this horrible moment." She shuddered again. "I can't even imagine. Unearthing a corpse!"

I took hold of Mom's arms, slipped from her hug and, before she could re-engage, took her hands in mine and held them firmly between us. "I'm fine, Mom. Matt and Doc Barnes just wanted to ask a few questions about what happened."

She swiveled to Doc Barnes. "Did you examine her for shock?"

"She's fine," he said.

"Mom," I said again. "Really, I'm fine."

She examined me anxiously, not ready to believe me. "You've always been the strong one," she finally said, acting like she wanted to hug me again.

"Mom, how did you even know?"

"Betsy called," Mom said, then swiveled to Matt. "And don't you be getting upset with Betsy. I've known her since forever. Besides, when a body is discovered, the mayor's office needs to be informed right away."

Very drily, Matt said, "Glad to see the

department is meeting the mayor's communications expectations, at least in this regard."

My ears perked up. Was I sensing tension between Matt and the mayor? I filed that away for future reference.

With concern for my emotional well-being at least temporarily allayed, my mom swung her attention to the hole in the wall.

"Is that…?" she began.

"How about we go upstairs?" I said, then looked at Matt. "Is that okay?"

"Please."

"Do you need me to stick around, or…?"

"Why don't you two go on home?"

"Of course. And will you…?"

He gave me a smile. "Yes, as soon as we know more."

"Which I'm guessing will be a while?"

He nodded. "It'll be a late night."

"You sure you don't want me to stay?"

"No need. I'll call if we have questions. How about I swing by tomorrow morning with an update?"

I'll admit I felt a flutter of anticipation at his words, along with a surge of gratitude. It had been a long afternoon and an even longer week. When the adrenaline wore off, I knew I'd want nothing more than to collapse in bed and let the world go black. Normally I don't respond well to being dismissed — and getting kicked out of my own building and told to be patient definitely counted as being dismissed — but this time felt different.

"Okay," I said, slipping my arm through my mom's. "We'll get out of your hair. See you tomorrow?"

"Tomorrow." His grey eyes held mine. "That's a promise."

CHAPTER 6

"*That's a promise.*"

His words echoed through me as Mom and I left my great-aunt's building and made our way to the spot on Main Street where Mom had parked her SUV. It wasn't the words themselves I was lingering over, or even how nice they sounded coming from him, but rather how they evoked echoes of the past — of the two years our paths entwined so joyfully and, in the end, painfully.

Dusk was settling in. I shivered as a gust of wind whipped through my hair. Though the autumn days still held hints of warmth, the nights were getting downright cold. Home barely a week and already I was back in sync with the rhythms of life in the town I'd once called home.

"You okay, Sarah?" Mom said, wrapping her

coat tighter around her neck, her heels clicking on the sidewalk.

"Yes," I replied, trying not to show impatience at having to answer the same question four times in just as many minutes. "What's the plan for dinner?"

"We still have leftovers, and I can make a salad."

"Sounds good."

We reached Mom's SUV and hopped in. She pulled out and I gazed out the passenger window as Main Street slipped by. Three blocks long and lined with shops and restaurants and other local businesses, the street was the heart of Eagle Cove. Built in the 1800s during the town's logging heyday, the downtown had never really been updated, giving it a Victorian-era time-capsule quality that, a century-and-a-half later, appealed to the tourists who flocked north in droves, eager for a taste of authentic New England charm.

These charm-seeking hordes were now Eagle Cove's economic lifeblood, keeping the local merchants busy and the town's five thousand residents employed. My gaze fell on the gold-and-red garlands wrapped around the street poles in anticipation of the upcoming Harvest Festival, just two weekends away. For more than twenty years, Aunt Emily had managed the festival's planning committee, delivering an annual event that was now one of the town's biggest draws.

But this year, she wouldn't be here for it.

I blinked back tears. The call had come out of nowhere eight days earlier, my sister relaying the shocking news that Emily's car had gone off the ridge road and tumbled down a chasm, killing her on impact and igniting a fire that burned everything inside. While the investigation was not complete, the working assumption was that the crash was an unfortunate accident.

I'd flown home right away and, together with my sister, taken charge of all the painful and necessary decisions that inevitably follow a loved one's death. The funeral, three days ago, had been packed with friends and neighbors whose outpouring of love and support had been gratifying, even overwhelming. Eagle Cove is a close-knit community, and my great-aunt had been a respected and much-loved mainstay.

Emily's death had hit Mom very hard. The two of them had been much more than niece and aunt — they'd been the best of friends. They'd relied on each other and enjoyed doing things together and saw each other (or at least talked) every day. For three days after the accident, Mom had barely left her bed. As the funeral approached, Grace and I had privately wondered whether Mom would be up for attending. It turned out our concerns were for nought: Mom had pulled herself together and rallied impressively, accepting the town's heartfelt condolences with composure and grace. She'd done Aunt Emily proud. At breakfast this morning, she'd surprised me by marching into the kitchen fully dressed and announcing she was ready to return to work. "Emily would forgive a week of mourning," she'd told me. "But she wouldn't approve of wallowing. Like she always said: Life must go on."

As indeed it must. With the downtown in our rearview mirror, Mom aimed us down the main county road toward the residential neighborhood I'd grown up in.

"I didn't know Matt was the new sheriff," I said.

"Going on two years now. I'm sure I mentioned it."

I sighed. "No doubt you did."

"Though I will say, there were a few times in the past year I avoided bringing him up."

"Because of…?"

"Yes, dear." She gave my arm a quick pat. "There was no point mentioning him while you were caught up in the divorce."

My gut told me I understood why, but I wanted to be sure. "Because mentioning Matt would be kind of like … rubbing salt in the wound?"

"Rubbing salt?" she repeated, her brow furrowing. "Oh, I see — because all those years ago, you let him go? No, that wasn't it. I just didn't want you distracted. Getting legally free and clear of that con-man husband of yours was your top priority, and rightfully so. And I know you. You're at your best when you focus."

I shook my head. "I really made a mess of things, didn't I?"

"What do you mean?"

"With everything. With my life."

"Don't you dare say that," she said instantly.

"I don't see why I shouldn't."

She shook her head. "Item one for the defense: Your wonderful daughter. No marriage, no daughter."

I smiled. Mom devoured legal shows like they were buttered popcorn and loved using courtroom jargon when arguing with me.

"I didn't have to get married for that."

"Oh, come now. That's not you and you know it."

She was right, of course — I'd always leaned traditional in that regard. "Okay, I'll give you that one. I have an amazing daughter."

"And you and that ex-husband of yours had some good years, before he became a crook."

"I suppose," I said reluctantly.

She took a left onto Maple Lane for the final minutes of the drive home. The neighborhood, built after the second world war for veterans and their families, featured a mix of ranch-style and two-story homes on small lots, with winding roads that rose and dipped with the natural contours of the hills.

I wasn't ready yet to abandon my self-flagellation session. "It's just — I was his wife. I should have known sooner."

She shook her head. "He fooled everyone, not just you. And don't you forget — we've talked about this. It's often the spouse who has the hardest time figuring things out, because the spouse has such a vested interest in everything being okay and good."

She was right about that, too, of course. The research showed it, which I knew because I'd read everything I could get my hands on about marriages in crisis while desperately searching for ways to survive the disaster in mine. On a rational level, I accepted what she was saying. But emotionally....

"The important thing," Mom continued, "is that you made it through. The divorce is final. You're free and clear. You're ready for your fresh start."

Fresh start. I cringed. Oh, how I disliked that phrase. What did it mean, actually and honestly? At the end of the day, wasn't *fresh start* just an empty, sugarcoated reminder that life was sometimes cruel and unfair and *not very nice*?

Hadn't my whole year been nothing but *fresh starts*?

A week after signing the divorce papers, my longtime employer (a large bank whose name I was determined to never utter again) had laid off my entire department. Sixteen years on the job had ended with a three-minute phone call, the H.R. rep's carefully scripted words — "displacement" the new favored euphemism for "you're canned" — escaping her mouth with all the warmth of an ice storm.

Two weeks after that blow, I'd helped my daughter Anna pack up her things and driven her five hours north to U.C. Santa Cruz to begin her freshman year of college. In her new dorm room, I'd helped her unpack, met her new roommate and, when it became clear that it was time for me to let my daughter go, given her a big hug, told her to call, and walked away with a cheerful wave and a proud smile on my face.

And when I got back to the car, I'd cried and cried and cried.

"Okay," Mom said as she pulled into our driveway, "we're home."

I realized Mom must have gone through the same wrenching experience when I'd left Eagle Cove all those years ago.

"I love you, Mom," I said.

She blinked, surprised. "I love you, too."

"I know I don't say that often enough. But I've resolved to do better on that front."

She shut off the car and gave me her full attention. "I'm glad to hear that."

"I miss her," I said, realizing as the words left my lips that I meant both Aunt Emily and Anna.

Mom patted my hand. "I do, too."

"I'm not going to let that dead body in the basement worry me."

"Good," she said. "Me either."

"No way Aunt Emily was involved," I added loyally, though in my heart I wasn't convinced of that.

"Of course not, dear." With that, Mom pushed open her car door and said, "It's been a long day. For both of us. Let's get you inside."

CHAPTER 7

I awoke the next morning in my childhood bedroom, in the same twin bed I'd slept in as a teenager. Sunlight streamed through the window, landing on the same desk I'd used for homework and reflecting off the same wall mirror I'd stood in front of anxiously every morning, wondering when I'd finally grow up and stop looking like a nerdy, frizzy-haired mess.

Pushing off the covers, I rolled out of bed and fell right back into my old morning routine, my feet making their way to the same spot in front of the mirror, where I found myself searching my face for flaws, my mouth shaping itself into the same disapproving frown.

A growl escaped my lips when I realized what I was doing. *Stop beating thyself up. Give credit where credit is due.* Like with my hair, which, after years of struggle, I'd finally figured out how to tame. Through careful styling, it now lay mostly straight, the coloring close to (but better than) my hair's natural brown.

With braces and pimples long gone, my face had turned out pretty decent as well, a reality I forced myself to acknowledge as I gazed upon my acceptable brown eyes, regular nose, normal lips, and mostly blemish-free skin.

The rest of me also fell into the good-enough category. I'd gained fifteen pounds during the divorce, but ten had been shed in the six weeks since Anna had left for college, thanks to the resurrection of my thrice-weekly running routine. Another five pounds and I'd be back to what I'd long ago accepted as my "regular" weight.

From downstairs, the familiar sound of a kitchen cabinet banging shut brought a smile to my lips. The house I'd grown up in was a two-story residence, with three bedrooms upstairs and a single bathroom that, during my teenage years, had been busier than Grand Central. Downstairs was a living room, dining room, kitchen, powder room, and pantry/laundry room that led to a two-car garage. From the dining room, sliding doors opened to a back deck overlooking a small yard. It was a modest home and a bit snug, but it was where I'd been raised and being inside it always lifted my heart.

I heard Mom talking with someone. Surely it

was too early for Matt to be here? I moved to the window and relaxed when I saw my friend Janie's car in the driveway.

Still, Matt could show up at any time....

A few minutes later, wet from the shower, I applied eyeliner and lip gloss and told myself I was getting made up because that's what I felt like doing today. Then I squeezed into my favorite pair of blue jeans (still a bit tight, but whatever) and a light blue blouse that made my figure look good.

I was about to head downstairs when I caught sight of a familiar packet of postcards poking up from the open suitcase on the floor. I'd brought the postcards with me from California on an impulse, grabbing them from my dresser and slipping them into my suitcase while still reeling from the news of Aunt Emily's death.

I picked them up and sat down on the bed, plucking at the ribbon holding the bundle together. The ribbon loosened and the postcards tumbled apart, their bright colors still vibrant even after all these years. Mailed to me by Aunt Emily during the years when she and Uncle Ted lived abroad — he'd worked for an oil company for thirty years — the postcards were among my most cherished mementos. When Emily found out how fascinated I was by her travels, she'd made a point of sending me a postcard from each place she visited. The arrival of each new card — from Dubai, Jakarta,

Caracas, or some other exotic locale I'd never heard of — sent me scurrying to the atlas to learn all I could.

Emily's international travels had ended when Ted died of a heart attack while stationed in Zurich. Suddenly alone at fifty-three and forced to reinvent herself, she'd surprised everyone by moving back to the small town she'd grown up in and opening a cafe.

The world's loss had been Eagle Cove's gain. I was twelve when Emily opened the cafe. It was really only then, at the start of the next great act in her life, that I got to know her. As a traveling aunt, she'd been a source of excitement and speculation and inspiration, but as the owner of Emily's Eats in the center of town, she became a real person. I grew to love and admire her for her strength, firmness, and kindness.

You lived such an interesting life, I thought. *And you were still going strong at eighty-three.*

Out loud, I said to myself, "I hope I take after you, Aunt Emily."

Carefully, I tied the postcards back up, returned them to my suitcase, and made my way downstairs.

CHAPTER 8

In the entry hallway I picked up my pace, drawn by the tempting aromas of bacon and eggs and the sounds of Mom and Janie chattering away.

"Morning." I stepped into the kitchen and made a beeline for the coffee pot.

Mom and Janie were at the small table near the back window, cups of coffee in hand. "What can I get you, dear?" Mom said, rising from her chair.

"Stay put." I grabbed a mug from an upper cabinet. "I got this."

Ignoring me, Mom bustled to the stove, where a pan of scrambled eggs and bacon lay waiting. "I'll fix you a plate."

Accepting the inevitable, I turned to Janie. "Hey, you. What brings you here?"

Janie pointed to a plate of scones on the table. "Testing a new recipe."

My stomach rumbled with anticipation. Janie's a superb baker — a true artist with cakes and muffins and cookies and scones. "Well, you know how happy I am to be your taste-tester."

Janie blushed, a shy smile lighting up her face. She's a kind woman, quiet and thoughtful by nature, with a lovely face and shoulder-length brown hair that she often pulls back into a ponytail while busy in the kitchen. We've been friends since sitting next to each other in Social Studies class in the eighth grade, shortly after she and her parents moved to town. After high school, she'd stayed on in Eagle Cove, working as a waitress and baker for several years before marrying a fireman named Ed and starting a family. Their twin boys, now grown up, had recently enlisted in the Army.

"It's a bacon-apple scone," she said. "I got the recipe from my friend Holly over in Heartsprings Valley and thought I'd give it a try."

With the mug of coffee warming my hands, I made my way to the table, picked up a scone, and took a bite. Immediately, my taste buds exploded with pleasure, the flavors rolling over my tongue.

"Oh, my," I burst out. "This is fantastic."

She smiled, pleased.

"Did I ever tell you you're a culinary genius?"

She laughed. "Only too often."

"I mean it. Genius."

Mom set a plate of eggs and bacon in front of

me and sat back down. "Janie's offered to help with the equipment inventory at the cafe."

"Oh," I said, taking a bite of eggs and adjusting to the shift in topic. "That's great. And thank you. But do you think we can get in there yet?"

"I don't see why not. The body was found in the basement, not on the ground floor."

She was probably right, but still....

Mom continued. "Betsy called. Matthew was there all night. They took out the body around midnight. Doc Barnes has already started on the autopsy."

"Betsy's quite a fount of information," I said drily.

"Oh, hush. You're glad to know and you know it."

She was right about that as well. After getting home the previous night, I'd taken one look at Mom's exhausted face and decided to hold off on any discussion of the body in the basement. Clearly, Mom's first day back at work had been hard on her. Which was completely understandable, because that's what grief does. It drains you, weighs you down, makes even the simple things difficult. The only way to get through it is to outlast it — to persevere until it fades. So after I helped Mom make a salad, we'd reheated a casserole, headed upstairs, and crashed.

I glanced at Janie. "I assume you heard?"

She nodded. "You're going to let Matt do his job, right?"

I tried to appear puzzled. "Of course. Why wouldn't I?"

Janie looked like she wanted to say something but was holding back.

Mom had no such qualms. "No nosing around. That's what we're saying."

"Mom...."

"It's better you stay out of this one."

"I get that," I said to placate her. "It's just ... I can't help but wonder."

Mom shook her head warningly.

"Like ... I wonder how long the body has been there. Janie, you worked for Emily at the cafe."

"Yes," Janie said cautiously.

"You were working there when she closed it."

"That's right."

"Was the closure a planned thing? A sudden thing?"

Janie frowned. "It was sudden. She called one morning and told us — me and the other staff — that she was shutting down. She gave us each a month's pay and apologized."

"And that was it?"

"Pretty much."

"Did she tell you why?"

"She said she needed to take a break. We

assumed it was a health issue that she didn't want to talk about."

I found myself nodding. It was a reasonable assumption, given that my aunt had been seventy-three at the time.

"Mom," I said, "what did Emily tell you?"

Mom frowned at me, irritated. "She told me she was ready for something new."

"That's it?"

"Of course." Clearly, the topic made her uncomfortable. "That's all there was to it. She wasn't ill, though it's understandable why everyone wondered at the time. No, she just decided to call it quits."

As the two of them waited for me to respond, a strange feeling washed over me. I got the strong sense they knew more than they were telling me — and that they'd decided to keep me out of the loop.

Before I could dig — and believe me, I had every intention of grabbing a shovel and going in deep — I heard the rumble of a truck engine.

Mom and Janie heard it, too.

"That must be Matthew," Mom said. "Sarah, why don't you let him in?"

CHAPTER 9

In the hallway, I used the wall mirror to check my face and teeth, even as I told myself I was being silly.

My gaze slid to a photo next to the mirror. The photo, part of Mom's hallway display of family pictures, showed four teenagers, arms entwined, grinning at the camera. We all looked so young — bursting with innocence and exuberance. At one end was Matt, on the other end Janie, and in the middle were me and Claire, my former best friend, the friend I once believed would be my best friend forever. Janie and Matt and I were wearing big smiles and Claire was laughing, her stringy blond hair as messy as always, her glasses perched haphazardly on her nose, her lanky figure still coltish and awkward. Snapped by Mom on a bright spring day, the photo captured the four of us in our final moments of adolescence. All too soon, we'd become adults. But in that last magical moment, we were still kids.

Two knocks on the door startled me out of my reverie. I took a deep breath and opened the door.

Matt stood there in the morning light, as tall and broad-shouldered as ever, and for a split second I flashed to the night of his senior prom, when he'd stood in the same spot in his rented tux, corsage box in hand, nervous and eager and ready to take his new girlfriend to the big dance.

He wasn't a kid any longer, but I sensed a bit of the same nervousness and eagerness beneath that handsome exterior.

"Hey," I said, pleased to hear my voice sound calm. "Come in."

"Thanks." He stepped past me — yes, definitely more solid now, but it all still totally worked — and nodded to the photo of the four of us. "I love this picture," he said with a grin.

"Me, too." Ignoring the flutter in my chest, I gestured toward the kitchen. "Janie and Mom are finishing up breakfast."

The two of them greeted him as he entered. "Let me get you some coffee, Matthew," Mom said, rising to her feet. "We have eggs and bacon, too."

When he didn't say no, I realized he was hungry and probably hadn't eaten. Under his sheriff's jacket he was wearing a different shirt — a blue button-down collared number — and his face was freshly shaved. Which meant he'd gone home and showered and changed before coming here.

A rebellious thought came: *Had he cleaned up for me?*

Don't be ridiculous, I immediately told myself. *Stop leaping.*

"You sure?" Matt said. "If it's no trouble."

"No trouble at all," Mom said. "Sit yourself down. Janie, he needs to try your new scone."

With a smile, Matt took a seat as ordered.

"It's a friend's recipe," Janie said as she handed him one. "Bacon-apple."

He brought it to his nose and sniffed, then took a bite and chewed slowly and thoughtfully, his face a mask of concentration.

His deliberations went on so long that I realized what he was doing.

"No teasing," I ordered him.

He broke into a grin and said to Janie, "This is awesome."

Janie blushed. "Really?"

"Just like everything you bake. You're a wizard. I love how the bacon and apple flavors enhance each other." He took another bite as Mom set a plate of eggs in front of him. "Thank you, Nancy."

Back in high school, Mom had been "Mrs. Boone" to him. Back then, their interactions had been defined by their relationships *with me*. But time had changed that. Now they both worked for the town. Now they were colleagues, maybe even friends.

I hadn't seen him in more than twenty years, but Mom and Janie probably saw him all the time. He was part of their lives and they were part of his.

And I wasn't.

I swallowed back a surge of emotion. I'd missed out on a lot when I'd left Eagle Cove all those years ago.

Matt took a bite of eggs, then said, "I promised an update."

"Yes," Mom said. "We're all ears."

He sat up straighter, transforming into the sheriff he'd become. "We removed the body last night, along with other evidence from the basement. Doc Barnes is performing an autopsy. The case is being investigated as a probable homicide."

We already knew that, thanks to Betsy, but we allowed him to tell us again.

"For now, the basement remains off-limits."

"What about the ground-floor cafe space?" Mom said.

"We've taped off some of the equipment for further analysis, but you're free to enter the space as needed."

"How late were you there?" Mom asked.

"Most of the night."

"You poor boy. You must be exhausted."

He gave her a quick smile. "Just part of the job."

I jumped in. "So who was the victim?"

"We don't know yet. He had no ID. We've sent off samples for DNA matching, but results will take time."

"How did he die?"

"We're waiting for the autopsy to confirm cause of death."

"The skin seemed kind of leathery," I said.

"Sarah," Mom said, irritated. "Do we have to go there?"

"It struck me as unusual," I said. "Isn't that right, Matt?"

I could tell what he was thinking: *Here we go again.* But what he said was, "We'll know more when the autopsy is completed."

"Which will be when?"

"Preliminary report later today, I hope."

"Will you share the results?"

He held my gaze. "We'll share what we can. I know you're worried about this. But I need you to let my department do its job."

Without nosing in, he didn't say.

"Of course," I said.

Three pairs of eyes stared at me, unconvinced.

"I promise!"

"We've heard that before," Mom muttered darkly.

"I have every confidence Matt and his team will do a great job."

"That's good," Mom said. "Because we have a lot to do today."

"What's on your agenda?" Matt asked.

"Janie's helping us with an inventory of the equipment in the cafe."

His gaze slid to me. "I hear Emily left you the downtown building, and your sister got her farm outside of town."

"That's right," Mom said, jumping in. "Emily was going to leave everything to me, but I told her I wanted it all to go to the girls."

He nodded sympathetically. "Sarah, I hear you're selling the building."

"That's right."

Though he didn't say anything, I sensed my answer disappointed him.

He checked his watch, shoveled more eggs and bacon into his mouth, then pushed out his chair and rose to his feet. "Sorry to rush, but I should get back downtown. Nancy, thank you for breakfast. Janie, thanks for the scone."

I stood up with him. "I'll show you out."

In the hallway a few seconds later, he paused, his hand on the door handle. "Can we talk privately for a minute?"

"Sure," I replied, my heart jumping.

We stepped onto the porch. I shut the door behind me. The morning air held a chill, but I felt the sun's warmth on my face.

He was gazing at me with an intensity I remembered vividly. "I didn't want to say more in front of the others," he said, his voice low. "But there are aspects of this case that worry me. I want you to be careful and stay safe."

"Stay safe?" I repeated.

"I know how you can be," he said, not giving an inch.

I offered what I hoped was a sunny, innocent smile. "You mean curious and determined?"

More like nosy and stubborn, I knew he was tempted to reply. But he said, "Sure, we can go with that."

"What are the aspects that concern you?"

He glanced at the closed door. "These details are not to be shared."

"Of course," I said, anticipation rising.

He took a deep breath, as if confirming with himself the wisdom of confiding in me, and then said, "The body's fingertips were burned off, along with the skin on the palms. Every tooth was pulled, and the face was smashed in."

I gasped. He'd relayed the information in a straightforward manner, but the reality he'd described was chillingly brutal. "Someone really wanted to make it hard to identify the body."

He nodded. "We've sent off DNA and I've asked for a rush, but we'll only get a match if the victim was already in the system."

My mind was racing as I considered the implications. "I get removing the fingerprints and the teeth, and even damaging the face. But burning the palms? That suggests his palms were scanned and recorded somewhere, which is not common. Maybe he worked at a place with high security? The kind of place that uses palm scans to identify and control who has access?"

"That's our working assumption."

"But there's nothing around here with that kind of security, at least not that I know of. Maybe a science lab or something over at Middlemore University?" I thought about Grace, who worked at the university as an administrator. Perhaps I could follow up with her?

Matt frowned, as if reading my mind. "I want you to leave the investigating to us. I'm sharing this with you because there's nothing run-of-the-mill about this man's death and I want you to be careful."

"I will be. Promise."

"I want you to stay out of it."

"Got it," I said immediately, trying to convey how on-board I was, though what he was asking was of course impossible. "So…. The removal of identifying features suggests the killer knew the victim, or at least knew who he was."

His frown deepened. Before he could change his mind about sharing more, I pushed on. "Do you know how he died?"

"Shot with a nail gun."

I blinked with surprise. "You mean, like a nail gun from a construction site?"

"Pressed against his chest. A single nail fired into his heart."

I shuddered, unable to avoid imagining the moment of death. The sound of the nail gun going off, the shock on the man's face, his body crumpling to the ground....

My distress must have shown because Matt said, "Sarah, I'm sorry. I shared too much."

"No, really, I'm fine," I said, though in that instant I wasn't.

"You sure?"

I took a deep breath, willing myself to calm down. "Positive," I said, with more certainty than I felt. "About the body not decomposing. Was it dried out?"

"The body was placed in a low-moisture environment for a period of time."

Immediately, I found myself doing a mental inventory of my aunt's building. Could anything there have been used to dry out the body?

With a jolt, I realized the answer was *yes*.

Reluctantly, I said, "On the ground floor, in the back of the cafe, my aunt had a commercial-grade food dehydrator. She used it to dry out fruits and make venison jerky. It's a pretty big unit. If you remove all the trays, it's probably large enough to hold a dead body."

"We know. We've examined it and collected samples for testing."

I swallowed. *And there it was.* A theory of the crime that laid out how a man could be killed, mummified, and buried, all within the confines of my great-aunt's building. A theory that aligned neatly with the physical realities of the corpse. The story of the man's death was getting clearer, and I didn't like where it was headed.

"How long was the body in the basement?"

"A decade, give or take. We'll have a more precise timeframe once additional tests are completed."

"So Aunt Emily was living in the building when the man was killed and placed in the basement."

He nodded.

"She shut down the cafe a decade ago," I continued. "Janie said she did it suddenly, without warning."

"Others have told us the same."

A wall of resistance was rising within me, even as the circumstances seemed to close in around my great-aunt. Given what was known, how could she not have been involved?

No, I told myself. *There's more to this. There has to be.*

"You can't really think Emily did this," I said. "Come on. You knew her."

His expression was sympathetic. "It's too early for conclusions." Then he took a deep breath and I realized he was leading up to something I wouldn't be happy about. "We'd like your permission to go through your aunt's apartment on the third floor and the vacant studio apartment on the second floor."

I inhaled sharply. It was a request I should have seen coming, but I hadn't.

I didn't respond right away. Tears threatened. I blinked and swallowed to push them back.

Matt's manner was apologetic, but the request was firm. If I didn't agree, he'd get a search warrant.

"Sure," I finally said, the words feeling like a betrayal. "Search away."

"Thank you."

"Will you do it today?"

"Yes. I should get over there now. We'll try to finish up this afternoon."

"If you need anything, Janie and I will be down on the ground floor doing an inventory."

"Thank you." He paused, then said, "Listen,

totally separate from the investigation, I'd love for us to catch up."

"I'd like that, too," I said, a jolt of pleasure — or was that anxiety? — rushing through me.

"Coffee?"

"Perfect."

"You're here ... how long?"

"For the next week."

"How about tomorrow afternoon?"

I blinked. He'd always been like this — direct and to-the-point and specific. "Sounds good."

"Okay," he said, a flush appearing on his cheeks. "Then...."

I realized he'd almost said: *Then it's a date.*

What he said instead was, "Tomorrow it is."

"Tomorrow it is," I repeated, feeling heat on my cheeks as well.

As he got into his truck and pulled away, I told myself I'd have to be careful. Past was not prologue. We were different people now.

And I needed to remember that.

CHAPTER 10

B ack in the kitchen, the first thing Mom and Janie did was pump me for intel about what Matt and I had been talking about. I told them the truth, or least part of it, sharing that he'd asked for permission to search Emily's apartment and the studio apartment on the second floor.

"Oh, gosh," Janie said.

Mom frowned but didn't react. Instead she said, "We should get going."

After loading plates into the dishwasher and wiping down the table and countertops, the three of us headed out.

Minutes later, with Mom behind the wheel and Janie following in her car, I said, "About Matt."

"What about him?"

"He said he wanted to catch up, have coffee."

"That's nice," she replied. "Right?"

"Oh, yes, totally." I took a deep breath. "When we catch up, what am I going to learn?"

"Well," Mom said as she turned off Maple Lane onto the county road. "His boys — one's a junior, the other a sophomore — are star athletes on the high school basketball and swim teams. The younger one's on the honors list. Very interested in science."

"That's great to hear."

"Matthew seems glad to be back in Eagle Cove, and enjoys being sheriff."

"Also good."

"The consensus around town is he's doing a good job. People like him. He hired a new deputy a few weeks ago. Deputy Martinez."

"I met her yesterday."

"The town council agreed to funding for two new hires, which pleased him."

I recalled a comment from the previous night. "Does he get along with the mayor?"

"Oh, sure," Mom said. "At least most of the time."

"Most of the time?"

"They both like being in charge. Which means sometimes there are … boundary disputes."

I smiled, liking how she'd phrased that.

"Minor stuff mostly," she continued. "Nothing to worry about."

I felt an itch of impatience. The information Mom was sharing was helpful, but....

"None of that's what you really want to know, is it?"

"Mom," I said automatically, preparing to disagree before stopping myself, because what was the point? "Okay, fine. Yes, get to the juice."

"He and his ex-wife finalized their divorce three years ago."

Now this was more like it. "Do we know why they...?"

"She left him. Met someone else. Remarried two years ago. Lives in Boston."

My eyebrows rose. "Wow."

"Not what you were expecting?"

"No." For a few seconds, I couldn't say anything, trying to wrap my head around that.

"She and Matthew were living in Nashua at the time. When he got the sheriff job here, they let the boys decide where they wanted to live, and they chose their dad and Eagle Cove."

"Wow."

"But the boys spend a fair amount of time in Boston as well."

"So the divorce was amicable?"

"Honestly, I have no idea. It was over and done with before he moved here. But my sense is the two of them managed it fairly well. The boys seem to be doing fine, and that's what's important."

"Have you met her?"

"No."

"So no sense of why...."

"No." She shot me a glance. "Now, you know I adore Matthew."

"Yes," I said, surprised by the direction she was taking the conversation.

"I imagine, in all fairness, it can't be easy being married to a police officer or a sheriff. The long hours, him getting called away in the middle of the night, worrying constantly about his safety...."

"Sure...."

"It must be very stressful. And there's nothing good about stress."

"Nothing at all."

"Maybe she was lonely as the only woman in a household full of men." She shuddered. "Let's face it, they're a different species."

I smiled. "Oh, come on."

"You know what I mean. You and Grace and I have interests in common. But boys.... What if they don't like the same things you like? What if they like things you don't understand or care about?"

"Sure, but...."

"Like, what's the deal with video games?" she said, her voice rising. "What's the point? Sitting there like zombies, staring at the TV, never going outside, never talking to people...."

I suppressed a smile. I didn't understand the appeal either, but Mom's opinion was obviously much stronger.

"What I'm saying is, maybe Matthew's ex-wife got lonely. Maybe…." She trailed off. "But what do I know? I never met her."

We'd reached downtown. Mom found a parking spot in front of my aunt's building and pulled in.

"One more thing," she said as she shut off the engine.

"What's that?"

"Sarah, I want to be as clear as I can be about this."

"About what?"

"I am not going to play matchmaker with the two of you."

I blinked, surprised. "Why is that?"

"Don't get me wrong. Matthew is terrific. I love him like the son I never had. But dating him comes with complications. Both job and family."

I swallowed back a surge of emotion. "And you're saying this to me because I have complications as well?"

Mom gave my arm a squeeze. "We all do, dear. An inevitable result of living. It would be terrific for you and Matthew to become friends again. That would be good for both of you. As for anything more…."

"Wait and see?"

Mom nodded.

"Time will tell?" I said.

"No need to rush into anything."

"Got it. And thank you." A thought came, and before I could stop myself, I said, "He's dating someone, isn't he?"

Mom paused before replying. "He's easily the town's most eligible bachelor. No getting around that."

That was hardly an answer. With difficulty, I restrained myself and waited for her to continue.

"From what I hear, he recently started seeing a gal named Cheryl who sells real estate in Larry's office. Nothing serious yet, but you never know."

And with that, she pushed open the door and hopped out of the SUV.

Face flushed, I followed suit, embarrassed that she'd known exactly what I'd wanted to know about the most.

I took a deep breath. Maybe Matt asking me out for coffee was really just about two people who'd once been close catching up after a long time apart. If so, that was actually fine. Preferable to any alternative, in fact.

Right?

Janie joined us on the sidewalk as we reached the cafe door.

I slipped the key in the lock, grabbed the handle, pushed open the door, and stepped aside, preparing myself to face whatever we'd find within.

"After you."

CHAPTER 11

Musty air washed over me as I followed Mom and Janie into the long-abandoned cafe. Flipping on the light switch, I let out a sigh. Superficially, aside from the dust and dropcloths and stacks of boxes, little had changed since my aunt had shut down the cafe a decade ago. The same row of booths ran along the wall opposite the same display counter and register, along with the same tables and chairs up front near the storefront windows. In the back, the kitchen and storeroom hadn't changed much either.

Janie had come prepared. She pulled a notepad from her purse, along with a pen.

She also had a newspaper, which she set down on the display counter near the register.

"This morning's *Gazette?*" I asked.

"Hot off the presses," Janie replied.

I moved closer, curious to see how it had changed. Published twice a week, *The Eagle Cove Gazette* was in many ways a typical small-town newspaper, its pages filled with coverage of town events and ads for local businesses. As a high school senior, I'd interned there for the editor-publisher, a man named Bob Underhill whose tenacity and fearlessness when reporting had made a big impression on a youthful me. "The pursuit of truth is noble, lonely work," he was fond of saying. "Power fears truth. Don't let power's minions stop you."

All of which was well and good, except for one thing: Bob had never met a conspiracy theory he didn't like. During my time as an intern, I'd gotten an earful — and then some — about all manner of corporate and government plots. He often used the *Gazette*'s editorial page to warn the town about secret nefarious schemes that only he could discern. Most folks had long ago decided to be amused by his rants, some even regarding them as a form of entertainment.

I picked up the paper and flipped to the masthead on the inside page. Yes, Bob was still there. He'd be in his late sixties now. I closed the paper and was about to ask Janie and Mom for an update when, in the right column on the front page,

I saw a headline I'd hoped I wouldn't: "Body Unearthed in Basement."

Oh, dear. My stomach clenched. The article was short and didn't include anything we didn't already know, probably because there hadn't been much time for reporting before the edition went to press. I scanned the byline — Wendy Danvers — and said to Janie, "Do you know the reporter, Wendy Danvers?"

"She's new. Moved here a few weeks ago. I've seen her around, but we haven't met."

"Mom?" I said. "Have you met her?"

"Oh, yes," Mom said. "Nice young woman."

"And Bob Underhill? How's he doing?"

"Oh, you know Bob. Same as always." She came over and read the headline, then sighed. "Guess it couldn't be helped."

"I hope he doesn't try to make some big conspiracy out of this."

Mom frowned. "He better not," she said darkly.

A realization came: Mom wasn't eager to talk about the body in the basement. Most of the time, she was chatty and inquisitive. But not when it came to this topic, most likely because talking about the body meant acknowledging the possibility that Emily had been involved in putting the body there.

As much as I wanted to dig into the mystery, Mom wasn't ready to hear about it. Around her, I'd need to tread lightly.

"So, Janie," I said, pointing to her notepad, "looks like you're raring to go."

She gave me a smile. "Every job needs a list."

"Where should we begin?"

She pointed toward the back. "Let's start in the storeroom and work our way to the front."

"Sounds good."

The cafe door's bell chimed and we swiveled to find Eagle Cove's mayor, Doris Johnson, stepping in and closing the door behind her.

"Good morning, everyone," she said warmly. An imposing woman in her late fifties, Mayor Johnson was a good four inches taller than me, with short black hair tinged with gray and smooth ebony skin that didn't show her age. I'd met her at the funeral, where she'd paid tribute to my aunt with a lovely, heartfelt address. After the service, I'd asked Mom about her and learned she'd first run for mayor five years ago, after thirty years as a middle-school teacher, and had recently won reelection in a landslide. According to Mom, she was a whirlwind of energy and kept everyone on their toes. "But in a good way," Mom said. "She's always exploring ways to promote the town."

"Do you like working for her?"

"Absolutely. With her, there's always something new. Once she sets her mind to something, there's no stopping her."

"What do you mean?"

"She does her homework. She figures out what needs to happen and who needs to do it before she even approaches you. It's like she maps out the battle plan, and like it or not you're getting drafted. She makes it impossible to say no."

Mom's assessment hovered in the back of my mind as the mayor approached.

"Sarah," the mayor said. "Do you have a few moments?"

"Of course."

"Thank you." Her gaze roved over the cafe before returning to me. "I'll get right to the point. Eagle Cove has an important request for you."

"For me?" I said, surprised.

She nodded. "Your great-aunt was an incredible woman. One of her many admirable qualities was her community spirit. Her dedication and commitment to our town were an inspiration to us all."

"Thank you." The mayor had said much the same at the funeral. But now her words were a warmup to something else.

Taking my hands in hers, Mayor Johnson aimed the full force of her no-nonsense gaze at me. "The Harvest Festival is in two weekends, right here on Main Street. I'm sure you remember the festival."

"Of course. I hear it's grown a lot in recent years."

"That's right — due in large part to your great-aunt, who managed the festival committee for many years and did so splendidly."

I frowned. "Surely you're not asking me to take her place?"

"Oh, no, no," the mayor hastened to assure me. "The festival committee has been preparing for the event for many months. All of that is well in hand."

"Then...?"

The mayor squeezed my hands for emphasis. "We need you to reopen the cafe."

A jolt went through me. "*What?*"

"Not in a permanent capacity," she said. "Just temporarily. During the festival weekend."

"Temporarily?"

"Think of it as a pop-up."

"A pop-up?" I was familiar with the concept — a chef renting a space for a few days or weeks, offering a special or experimental menu, then closing up and moving on — but the idea that I could do that was, quite simply, *crazy*.

"Nothing fancy or complicated," the mayor continued. "We need a place to sell coffee, tea, cider, hot chocolate, that sort of thing, along with baked goods — muffins, scones, cookies, and the like."

"What about Mario's? They already have coffee and biscotti."

"Mario himself suggested this option," she said. "Last year, the line for morning muffins and coffee extended out the door and interfered with his lunch service. He needs his kitchen and staff to focus on their regular menus."

"What about carts outside for coffee and treats and such?"

"We'll have those as well, but we've learned over the years that they're not enough."

I withdrew my hands from the mayor's firm grip and took a step back. "Well," I said, "I don't know how that would even be possible. There's simply too much to tackle, and not enough time, and…."

The mayor fixed me with a patient stare but didn't say a word.

I realized what she was doing. She was waiting for me to list my objections so she could bat them down, one by one. Maybe I could out-silence her? Almost immediately, as I took in her patient, implacable demeanor, I knew that tactic wouldn't cut it.

I sensed a certain inevitability to what was about to unfold, but I wasn't going down without a fight. "I don't know a thing about cafes. Or baking, for that matter."

"Luckily, you know people who do." The mayor gestured toward Janie. "Janie is a wonderful baker, has a part-time catering business, and worked for your aunt when the cafe was open."

I glanced at my friend. "I couldn't possibly ask her to sign up on such short notice for something so huge."

To my surprise, Janie gave me a sheepish shrug. Which told me two things: Not only had the mayor already talked with Janie, but Janie was *on board*.

I now understood what Mom and Janie hadn't told me back at the house. They'd known this ambush was coming.

Torn between admiration for their preparation and annoyance about not being approached first, I swung back to the mayor. "I see you've already begun recruiting the team."

A smile flickered briefly across the mayor's face, but she didn't reply, her gaze unwavering.

"As I'm sure you heard," I said, retreating to my next line of defense, "I'm selling the building."

"Yes," she said. "Do you have a buyer yet?"

"No."

"Any expressions of interest yet?"

"No."

"Have you selected an agent to help with the sale?"

"No."

"Even if someone walks in today with a perfect offer, completing a sale takes time. Certainly longer than the ten days between now and the Harvest Festival."

She was right about that, of course. But I wasn't ready to give in.

"I don't even know if I'm legally able to do what you ask. What with the will and probate and...."

"Jim," the mayor said, referring to Jim Atkins, my aunt's lawyer, "knows how important the festival is to the town. You should give him a call."

Which meant she'd already spoken with Jim and determined there was nothing legal getting in the way of me doing what she wanted.

I had three cards left. "This place is a mess. I have no idea what's here, or what condition the equipment is in, or...."

"I'll have Barney — he's the building inspector — come by first thing tomorrow."

"And if he finds something we have to fix?"

"Then I'll have the Gundersons" — the family who ran the town's hardware store — "come over right away." Before I could bring up the potential costs, she added, "The festival has a rainy-day fund for unexpected but necessary operational expenses. I'm sure the committee will agree to pay part of the expenses for any repairs needed to get the cafe ready for the festival."

"The town will help pay for necessary repairs?"

"Within reason, yes, and nothing excessive. The good news for you is that any repairs needed for the festival will also likely be needed to get the building prepped and readied for sale."

"And you'll help with permits and things like that?"

"Oh, of course."

"What about the investigation?" I said, playing my second-to-last card.

"That, of course, is up to the sheriff. It's likely the basement will remain off-limits for now. But he's given us the go-ahead to clean up the cafe and get it ready for business."

Which left one last card: *me*.

"Madam Mayor," I began.

"Please, Sarah, call me Doris."

"Doris," I said, collecting my thoughts. "I very much appreciate the thought and preparation you've put into this."

I paused, waiting for her to say something. But she didn't, instead allowing silence to fill the room.

Next to me, I sensed Janie and my mom gazing at me anxiously.

"Here's the thing," I said. "I've been here for over a week already, and I really need to get back to California."

The mayor said, "I understand completely. I'm told you have a ticket to fly back next week, two days before the festival weekend."

"That's right," I said, forcing myself to not glare

at my mom, who was obviously the source of the mayor's intel.

"I also understand your daughter Anna is planning to come home for a weekend."

"That's right."

"The weekend *after* the Harvest Festival weekend."

"That's right."

"Nothing is more important than family," the mayor said. "I would never ask you to do anything that gets in the way of time with your daughter. But I am asking you now, on behalf of the town of Eagle Cove, to help your community by opening the cafe for the festival. You'll need to push back your departure by a few days — the town will pay for any airline change fees — but we will make sure you're home for your weekend with your daughter."

I appreciated the way the mayor framed her request — in particular, what she'd chosen *not* to say. No doubt Mom had also shared that I was recently divorced and recently laid off and had nothing but an empty house to go back to. But the mayor hadn't mentioned any of that. She'd kept her pitch positive by appealing to my community spirit, and sweetened the request with a promise to help pay for repairs.

Besides, I realized, it sounded like Janie wanted to do it. And if I could help my friend….

"Janie," I said. "You sure you're up for this?"

"Absolutely," Janie replied immediately, her face brightening with anticipation.

I turned back to the mayor. I'd been played by a pro, but somehow I didn't mind.

"Congratulations," I said, accepting my fate with as much grace as I could muster. "You've got yourself a temporary cafe."

CHAPTER 12

With a warm smile and a big hug, Mayor Johnson thanked me and, after promising the town's full support and cooperation, swept out of the cafe with Mom in tow.

In her wake, a wave of doubt rolled in.

What in the world had I just signed up for?

I enjoy challenges, at least most of the time. Throw something at me and chances are good I'll run with it. But a task of this magnitude? Clearing away a decade of disuse and establishing a working cafe in barely a week? The musty, dusty space seemed to close in around me. Panic creeped in and unsheathed its claws, preparing to pounce.

I whirled on Janie. "You knew this was coming."

Guilt flashed across her face. "I'm sorry," she said, obviously distressed. "I wanted to tell you, but...."

I softened immediately. I'd always found it impossible to be upset with Janie — she was easily the kindest person I knew.

With a sigh, I said, "Oh, I get it. The mayor wanted to be the one who asked."

She gazed at me anxiously. "Are you okay with this?"

"I don't like being the last to know, but otherwise ... I guess so?"

My answer brought a tentative smile. "It's a lot of work, but I think it's going to be fun."

"Oh, do you now?" I returned her grin. "We'll see how you feel in a day or two, when we're both sweaty and dirty and stinky and every muscle in our body is aching."

Her smile grew wider. "That's my idea of heaven."

I laughed. "Well, since we now have a pressing deadline, we better dive in."

We began by coming up with two lists, one for "must-do" tasks and another for "if-we-have-time" items. Steadily and methodically, starting in the storeroom, we moved our way toward the front. We'd always worked together well, going back to prom committee in high school. Instinctively, we understood each other's rhythms.

As the lunch hour approached, we'd finished in the storeroom and had advanced into the kitchen. It wasn't a large space, but the layout was good, with appliances and countertops along the walls and a large stainless-steel prep island in the center. In a corner, I noticed what appeared to be a vertical air duct in the wall with a wooden door at counter level. Curious, I grabbed the door handle and pulled it up. I inhaled in surprise — I'd discovered what appeared to be an air shaft.

"Janie," I said, peering in. "What is this?"

"Oh, that's the dumbwaiter," she said. "Back when the building was built, they used it to move stuff up and down between the floors."

"Does it still work?"

"Not sure. We never used it. I don't know if the elevator cart — I'm not sure what you call it — is even still there."

I searched for a handle or button or pulley but didn't find anything. "Does the shaft go all the way down to the basement?"

"And up to the third floor."

"These old buildings are full of fascinating nooks and crannies."

Janie returned her attention to our lists. "That's one way of putting it."

I joined her in perusing our tasks. "Our list is awfully long, isn't it?"

"It'll work out," she said. "Just you wait and see."

"I admire your optimism."

She gestured to the first of the kitchen's two gas ovens. "Ready for our next task?"

I sighed, then bent down and grabbed the bottom of the oven. We were hoping the oven was on rollers — an expectation we were about to put to the test. "Ready."

Janie reached across the counter and took hold of the back of the oven. "One, two, three —"

We pulled, doing our best to inch the oven away from the wall. After a few seconds of resistance, we got movement.

"More," I said.

The second pull yielded several more inches. "Is that enough?"

"Let me see." Carefully, I climbed up onto the counter, grabbed my flashlight, and aimed the beam downward.

As light flooded the space behind the oven, I swallowed back a rush of emotion. Just yesterday, my trusty flashlight had discovered a *corpse*. Crazy to think of that happening here, in this very building. I wondered if Matt and his deputies had found anything upstairs. I'd heard them heading up and down a few times, but so far hadn't seen them.

"Everything seems okay," I said, "but the gas connector tubes are old. We'll need a plumber to replace them before we turn on the gas."

"Got it." Janie grabbed the notepad and added yet another task to our must-do list.

From up front, a familiar voice yelled, "Who's back there?"

Gabby bustled into the kitchen, cane at the ready, wearing a vibrant orange-and-green floral print dress. She surveyed the scene, scowling at the oven we'd just pulled out from the wall. "Digging for another dead body?"

"Gabby," I said, ignoring her question as I carefully climbed down from the counter. "Good to see you. I have news."

"You mean the news about you and Janie doing a pop-over?"

It took me a second, but I got it. "A pop-up cafe, yes. For the festival. How did you hear?"

Gabby waved the question away. "I have my sources." To Janie, she said, "You're in charge of the baking, right?"

"Right," Janie said.

"Good." She shot me a stern look. "Follow Janie's lead and you'll be fine."

Unsure whether to be amused or insulted, I changed the subject. "Are the sheriff and his deputies still upstairs?"

Gabby's scowl returned. "What do they think they're going to find up there, a pot of gold?"

"How late were they here last night?"

"Midnight. Kept asking questions." Then she added, in the same faux-innocent tone she'd used the previous day, "I had no answers, of course, since I don't know a thing."

"Of course not," I said, with a hint of skepticism that I probably should have hidden.

She snorted and said to Janie, "You've got your hands full with this one. All those years in the California sunshine have overheated her brain."

I gave her a smile. "I apologize in advance for any construction noise. We have updating to do to get everything ready."

"Don't you worry about that. It'll be nice to have the cafe running again. The girls and I can't wait."

I wasn't sure who "the girls" were, but I imagined a gang of cane-wielding octogenarians, each as spirited as their indomitable ringleader. I was about to ask for details when I heard a sound behind me and gasped as a cat emerged from the dumbwaiter shaft. He was large and sleek, with orange fur that practically begged to be touched. With athletic ease, he stepped onto the counter, then hopped down to the kitchen floor.

"Who is this?" I said, instantly smitten, bending down and extending my hand.

"Mr. Snuggles," Gabby said.

My brow furrowed. Surely a cat this proud and regal deserved a tougher name, or at least one less cutesy?

Mr. Snuggles made a beeline for me, his gait confident and easy. A few inches from my outstretched hand, he paused to give me a thorough inspection. Then, apparently deciding I passed muster, he leaned in and rubbed his face against my hand. His soft fur felt wonderful on my fingers. Before I knew it, he'd slipped beneath me and was rubbing himself against my legs, purring loudly.

"He's so friendly!" I said with a gasp.

"When he wants to be," Gabby allowed.

"Is it okay if I pick him up?"

Gabby shrugged. "He'll let you know."

I picked up Mr. Snuggles and held him in front of me, his gaze level with mine, letting him decide if he was comfortable with me. He regarded me intently for a few seconds before stretching forward and pressing his nose against my chin, his whiskers tickling my cheek.

"You are so adorable," I said.

I shifted him into my arms. He relaxed into me and started purring loudly.

"I'm beginning to understand his name."

Gabby was assessing me carefully, as if judging my performance on a crucial test.

"How old is he?"

"Five, we think."

"You think?"

"He was a stray. Just showed up one day."

"And you took him in?"

When she blinked uncomfortably, I realized something: Gabby's fondness for this feline charmer made her feel self-conscious, perhaps even vulnerable. Beneath her crusty demeanor, had I caught a glimmer of a secretly affectionate heart?

I heard a noise and swiveled to see Mr. Benson at the kitchen door. "Oh, there he is," he said, referring to Mr. Snuggles.

"I take it he's yours?"

"Yes," Mr. Benson and Gabby said at the same time.

They glared at each other before Mr. Benson said, "I feed him in the mornings."

"I do evenings," Gabby said.

Mr. Benson sighed. "The truth of the matter is, Mr. Snuggles has the run of the building and relies on both of us."

I smiled. "The entire building?"

"Basement to top floor."

"Including the dumbwaiter shaft?"

"He's a born climber. It's his favorite way of getting from floor to floor."

I thought about my aunt and her third-floor apartment. "Were Aunt Emily and Mr. Snuggles buddies?"

"Very much so," Mr. Benson said. "He loved her, and she him."

"He doesn't show the love to just anyone,"

Gabby added, still eyeing me. "His standards are very high."

"Well, I think he's wonderful," I said as his purrs vibrated through me.

I heard another sound up front, and a second later, Matt and Deputy Martinez made their way into the kitchen.

Suddenly the space seemed very full.

"Welcome to the party," I said.

Matt surveyed us for a second. "Everyone, glad you're all here. I have an announcement. We've tentatively identified the man in the basement."

The room went still. I breathed in sharply. "That was fast."

"Unusually fast. I called in a favor to have our sample tested right away, and we got lucky — a match was already in the system."

His gaze settled on Mr. Benson and Gabby. "The man has been identified as one Peter Messina."

Mr. Benson blinked, and Gabby arranged her face into a puzzled frown.

"Gabby, Donald, do you remember meeting him?"

"Peter Messina, you say?" Mr. Benson said cautiously. "I don't believe so."

"Nope," Gabby said.

"He was married to a woman named Amy Messina."

"Amy Messina," Mr. Benson repeated slowly, as if searching his memory for the name.

Gabby tried to appear even more puzzled.

A twitch in Matt's lips told me he wasn't buying their act any more than I was, but his tone remained neutral. "According to records we found upstairs in Emily's apartment, Amy Messina was, for a brief period ten years ago, a tenant in this building, in the studio apartment on the second floor."

"Is that so?" Mr. Benson murmured. "Now that you mention it, I vaguely recall a young lady who was here briefly…."

"Quiet little thing," Gabby said. "Kept to herself."

"Can you describe her?" Matt asked.

"Mousy, brown hair," Gabby said. "Skinny. Maybe thirty? Seemed shy, maybe even scared."

"Scared?" Matt said.

"Just a sense. She wasn't here long. I don't think we ever even spoke."

Matt said to Mr. Benson, "Donald, what about you? Did you ever talk with her?"

Mr. Benson shook his head. "I don't believe so. Sorry."

"Did Emily ever say anything about Amy?"

"Not to me," Gabby said.

"Nor I, Sheriff," Mr. Benson added.

Matt must have felt frustrated, but he hid it well.

"Janie, Sarah, either of you ever meet or hear anything about Peter or Amy Messina?"

"Not a thing," I said, completely truthfully.

"Sorry, Matt," Janie said. "Emily often let people stay in the studio apartment, sometimes for just a few days. If Amy wasn't here long, I doubt I would have met her."

Gabby chimed in. "Janie's right. There's always someone new in the studio apartment."

"That was Emily through and through," Mr. Benson said. "A very generous woman. Why, just last month, when Sally and Joe's remodel was behind schedule and Joe's brother and wife visited, Emily let them stay here."

Gabby fixed Matt with an accusatory glare. "So you can't expect us to remember some tiny slip of a girl from a decade ago."

"Frankly," Matt replied, his voice level and even, "I'm surprised you recalled anything at all. You never met her, never spoke with her, she was barely here for any time at all — yet your memory of her was vivid enough to provide us with important details."

Gabby went still as she realized her mistake. "What are you saying?" she said, the grip on her cane tightening.

"Nothing," Matt said mildly. "But I'd like you to sit down with Deputy Martinez and work on a sketch."

"Me?" Gabby said. "Why?"

"We might get lucky. The deputy is a talented artist. A sketch of Amy Messina might jog some memories."

Gabby glowered at him, but what could she do but agree? After a few tense seconds, she let out a sigh of reluctant cooperation. "When?"

"Now. Deputy Martinez can drive you to the station and back home when you're done."

Gabby swiveled toward me. "Sarah, if I'm not back soon, call my lawyer and tell him I'm being involuntarily and unlawfully detained by your once-and-future sweetie-pie."

I blinked, unsure I'd heard correctly. My once-and-future *what*?

Matt's eyes widened with surprise. Behind him, Deputy Martinez was staring at Gabby like she'd discovered a space alien. Clearly the frail, uncertain woman she'd met the previous night wasn't aligning with this robust version.

"Jim Atkins," Matt said to me, a hint of mischief in his tone.

"Jim what?"

"Jim is Gabby's lawyer."

"How do you know that?"

"Jim is everyone's lawyer."

"And a darn tootin' good one, too," Gabby said. She whirled on Mr. Benson. "Take care of my cat, you old crank."

"Woman, I —"

Gabby cut him off with a wave of her cane and turned to Deputy Martinez. "Let's go," she said, shuffling away with vigor. "And don't try sticking me in the back seat. I'm sitting up front!"

CHAPTER 13

Thankfully, Gabby's departure launched an exodus from the kitchen. Mr. Benson took Mr. Snuggles from my protesting arms and headed upstairs. Matt left with Gabby and Deputy Martinez, but not before letting me know that the search of the studio and Emily's apartment was complete.

Janie, bless her heart, didn't say a word about Gabby's "sweetie-pie" crack, though an amused smile flitted across her lips when she caught my attention lingering on Matt as he left the kitchen.

We returned to the inventory with a vengeance, adding task after task before popping across the street to Mario's for a late lunch — lasagna for me, fettucine alfredo for Janie. Then, with hot lattes warming our hands, we headed back to the cafe and settled into a table near the storefront window to tackle our next step: organizing the to-do items into a rough schedule.

As I scanned our tasks, I let out a groan. We had a mountain of work ahead of us. Before pouring a single cup of coffee or baking a single scone, we had gas lines and appliances to test, lighting to check and replace, stacks of boxes to open and sort and move, floors and walls and storage cabinets to scrub, and so much more. If any major appliances didn't work, we'd have to repair or replace them. If we lacked any necessary baking or cooking or serving items, we'd need to beg, borrow, or steal to get them. Most worrying to me was the lingering musty smell: I really hoped it came from dust and dirt and grime and not from a leaky pipe in the wall.

Or another dead body.

I frowned, annoyed that I'd allowed the thought to cross my mind.

Focus on the cafe, I ordered myself. *Now is not the time for investigating.* With the festival looming, the pressure was on. Besides, as much as I itched to dig into the mystery of the dead body in the basement, I didn't see how I could help at this point. Matt seemed to be making good progress. When we met for coffee tomorrow — my stomach fluttered at the thought — he'd doubtless have more to share.

I gazed across the table at Janie. Despite the long morning and afternoon we'd just pushed through, she seemed happy, energized, in her element. Without question, she was exactly the right partner to join me in this insane endeavor, her patience and quiet optimism the balm I needed to keep me calm and focused.

"You are so great," I said to her.

She gave me a smile. "Right back atcha."

"I don't know about that. I'm not sure what I bring to this."

"Don't say that."

"You have the baking and cafe expertise to pull this off. I'm just a laid-off former corporate drone."

Janie shook her head. "You're an excellent organizer, for one thing." She pointed to the schedule. "See?"

I sighed. "Let me know how you're feeling in two days, when we're knee-deep in this and the clock's a-ticking."

"Anything comes up, we'll talk it through."

I gave her a grateful smile. "Listen, about the talking thing. I know I haven't been good at communicating, especially the last few years. Going forward, I promise to do better. Beginning with telling you how much I appreciate you and love you and value our friendship."

Her eyes got misty. "You've always been one of my closest friends and you always will be. You and Claire were my lifelines when I moved here."

I gazed at her fondly. "I don't deserve you."

"Oh, stop," she said, but I could tell she was pleased.

"Speaking of She Who Shall Not Be Named," I said, referring to Claire, "have you heard anything lately?"

She shook her head. "Not lately. When she was here a few years ago, we had dinner. How about you?"

"It's been four, maybe five years. She was in L.A. on business. We had lunch." I frowned at the memory. As bad as I was at keeping in touch, Claire was worse. After college, she'd basically cut me and Janie out of her life. Twenty years later, I still didn't know why.

"She didn't reach out when you were going through the divorce?"

"Nope."

"I'm sorry to hear that."

"I am, too." I took a sip of latte, ignoring the sting of resentment and betrayal I felt whenever I thought about my former best friend. "Though in all fairness, even if she had reached out, I probably wouldn't have been ready or able to share."

Janie's gaze was steady. "Something's on your mind."

I nodded. "Only that time really does fly. I haven't lived in Eagle Cove in twenty-five years, yet in some ways it feels like I was here yesterday."

Janie's gaze roved over the cafe. "Being in here again brings back a lot of memories."

"Good ones, I hope?"

"Oh, definitely. Emily's Eats was a wonderful place to work."

A surge of sadness hit me, but I managed to push it back. "I can't believe my aunt is gone."

"She talked about you and Claire a lot."

Claire again. "They always got along really well."

My mind went to the row of condolence cards on the mantel in Mom's living room. Among them was a beautiful card, postmarked Washington, D.C., in which my former best friend had written, "Nancy, Sarah, and Grace, please accept my deepest condolences for your loss. I loved Emily and will always be grateful I had her in my life. She was an inspiration to me and countless others. I will remember her always with admiration and appreciation. With all my love, Claire."

My former best friend hadn't come to the funeral. Not that I'd expected her to.

Though I'd wanted her to.

I swallowed back another surge of emotion.

Because I missed her.

Which was only half-right.

Because I really, really, really wanted to yell at her and find out why she'd cut me out of her life.

Now *that* had the ring of truth. A smile came to

my lips, which Janie noticed. "Penny for your thoughts?"

"I'm imagining chewing out Claire for abandoning us in favor of her fancy high-powered life in D.C."

Janie smiled. "Fancy? High-powered?"

"Well, busy. The life of a corporate consultant has a certain glamour, I suppose?"

"Maybe," Janie said. "Though I have to say, it also sounds…."

I waited for her to finish. When it came to expressing anything negative, especially about people she knew and loved, Janie struggled.

"Lonely," she finally said. "Last I heard, she wasn't dating."

"The divorce from Ben was, what, six years ago?"

"Seven, I think."

"Time really does fly. Do her parents still have the farm on Old Winstead?"

"They retired to Florida a few years ago, but they kept the farm. They rent it out to tourists."

I was about to ask more when a knock on the front window startled me.

Jerry Meachum, the plumber whose leaky pipe speculation had led to me bashing in the basement wall, was standing on the sidewalk outside, an apologetic expression on his round face.

"Jerry!" I said, waving him to the door. "Come in."

He made his way inside. Back when we were kids, Jerry had been ungainly and shy. Now he was *large*, ungainly, and shy. Dressed in corduroy overalls over a blue flannel shirt, with a blue windbreaker and a Red Sox cap on his balding head, he seemed even more uncertain than usual. "Sorry to bother you two," he said. "Is this an okay time?"

"Of course. Pull up a chair."

Gabby hadn't been wrong about Jerry being on the dim side. He'd struggled at school, but his earnest nature and willingness to keep trying had earned him a diploma. After high school, he'd gotten a job at the hardware store and found work in construction and plumbing. Mom assured me he had a reputation for steadiness and reliability.

He moved a chair to the end of the table and settled in. "I hear you're opening the cafe for the festival."

"That's right," I said.

"You need help, let me know."

"Thanks. Don't be surprised if we take you up on that. We've been working on our to-do list, and it's long."

"Can I see?"

Janie slid him her notebook and he read through the lists slowly.

After absorbing the tasks, he looked up at me.

"Did you find a leaky pipe in the basement yesterday?"

"No. But I'm guessing you heard what I did find?"

"Oh, yeah. Everybody's talking about it."

Of course everybody was. Eagle Cove lived for gossip.

"I'm sorry about that," he said.

"Sorry? Why?"

His tone was anxious. "Because I'm the one who told you about the pipe maybe leaking."

"And?"

"It's my fault you went digging."

"Oh, I see."

"It must have been bad, finding the body."

"Definitely a shock. But I'm fine."

"Really?" he said, still not convinced.

"Promise — totally fine." I knew he wouldn't stop worrying about me until I distracted him, so I said, "What are they saying?"

"Who?"

"Everybody. You said everybody's talking about the body."

"Oh, yeah. They're saying it was that guy."

A jolt went through me. "What guy, Jerry?"

"The guy who barged in wanting Amy."

Whoa. My heart started beating faster. Jerry knew something — but what?

"Barged in? Where?"

"Here," he said as if that was obvious, which maybe it was.

"When?"

"The day before Emily shut down the cafe."

Double whoa. I made an effort to keep my voice calm. "Were you here that day?"

"Oh, yeah. It was lunchtime. I was having a burger and fries. This place always had the best burgers."

"What did the guy say?"

"He said, 'Where's Amy?'"

"Was he upset?"

"Oh, yeah."

"Worried? Angry?"

Jerry's brow furrowed. "Kind of both?"

"Was Amy here?"

He shook his head. "She was at the grocery store."

"Who did he ask?"

"He asked Emily."

I swallowed. "What did Emily say?"

"Emily grabbed him by the arm — you know, like she did when she wanted to give you a talking-to? — and took him outside. We couldn't hear what she said, but she was angry."

"What happened then?"

He shook his head. "Don't know. He went away. Never saw him again."

"What happened when Amy came back from the store?"

He frowned. "Emily said something to her and she went upstairs."

"And then?"

"That's it." He stared at me uncertainly, like he was aware I wanted more but was unsure how to provide it.

I glanced at Janie. "Do you remember this?"

Janie was slowly shaking her head. "I don't think so."

"You were out that day," Jerry said. "The twins were sick."

"Ah," Janie said.

"Jerry, does Matt know about this?"

"Oh, yeah. He came by the hardware store and I told him."

For a few seconds, I allowed the information to roll through my head. "So you met Amy."

"Sure," he said. "Just a bit."

"What was she like?"

He thought for a moment. "She was quiet. Maybe … sad?"

I nodded. His description aligned with Gabby's.

"Did Matt ask you to help with a sketch?"

"I'm going to the station now."

Janie glanced at her watch. "I should be heading out, too. Ed has the night shift, so I'm making an early dinner."

I rose to my feet. "Jerry, thanks for stopping by. I'll probably be giving you a call."

"Got it," he said, standing up. "See you guys later."

As the door shut behind him, I swiveled to Janie. "If you leave the notebook with me tonight, I can get everything into a spreadsheet."

"Thanks," she said with a smile. "Want me to pick you up at your mom's house tomorrow?"

"Sure. Nine?"

"Need a ride home?"

I shook my head. "Mom will swing by later. Right now, I'm heading upstairs to Emily's apartment."

CHAPTER 14

As I trudged up to the third floor, each step a reminder of how tired I was, I found myself wondering what I would find inside my aunt's apartment. I fully expected that Matt and his deputies had treated the place with respect during their search — but what if they hadn't? What if they'd tossed the joint? What if I walked in and found drawers pulled out, couch cushions ripped apart, artwork knocked off walls, papers scattered everywhere?

All seemed fine in the third-floor hallway. I unlocked my aunt's door and flipped on the light switch. A quick inspection of the entry foyer revealed complete and utter normalcy — no mess in sight.

When I caught my reflection in the wall mirror above the sideboard, I shook my head with dismay:

The only mess in the apartment was *me*. Today's inventory had taken a toll. My cheeks were pale and drawn. My hair looked dirty, even oily. My favorite blue blouse had a smudge on the front.

I switched off the light, set the keys on the antique oak sideboard, and made my way across the darkened living room to my aunt's rocking chair near the front windows. The chair was a classic Boston rocker with a spindled back that I knew felt surprisingly good when pressed against sore back muscles. After running my fingers over the chair's polished oak curves, I settled in with a grateful groan. From this spot, I had a view of Main Street below and, in the distance, the forested ridge surrounding Eagle Cove. Across the street, the neon sign in Mario's window flickered in the dusk.

I'd always loved this apartment. A graciousness pervaded these well-proportioned rooms with their high ceilings, large windows, and easy flow. Most of the original Victorian trim and moldings remained, along with the original wide-plank oak flooring. Somehow, the apartment conveyed contentment, like it was pleased with how well it had been treated over the years.

Indeed, my aunt's careful imprint was everywhere. She had always been clear and deliberate in her life choices — an approach reflected in how she'd decorated the place. There was a spareness, a precision, to her curated mix of midcentury and antique furnishings. If a piece wasn't both beautiful and functional, it didn't make the cut. The art pieces — paintings and sketches mostly, covering a range of styles and subjects — were similarly well-considered, each piece positioned far enough from the others to allow it room to breathe.

There was one big exception to this uncluttered aesthetic: On the longest wall in the living room, my aunt had hung dozens and dozens of framed photos, arranging them — cramming them — together in a happy jumble. Nearly every photo on her "travel wall" showed her and Uncle Ted in a place they'd visited during their years overseas.

I rose from the rocker, switched on the table lamp next to the sofa, and stepped closer for yet another glimpse into my aunt's adventurous past. What a life she'd lived! It was hard to pick a favorite snapshot, though I was partial to one of Emily at a market in Marrakesh, twirling for the camera as she showed off a vibrant red shawl, the shop merchant laughing with delight. I also adored a candid photo of her and Ted at a formal dinner in Hong Kong, chopsticks in hand, staring with trepidation at the plate of chicken feet that a waiter had just placed in front of them. "We ate them, of course," Emily told me when I'd asked about that moment. "To refuse would have been rude. Fortunately, they proved delicious."

Over the years, my aunt's hair had gone from brown to gray to white, and her face had acquired the usual inevitable wrinkles. But otherwise she'd remained much as she appeared in these photos: tall and thin, upright and confident, moving through life with decisiveness and vigor. Her face — angular and striking rather than conventionally beautiful — framed expressive hazel eyes that had seemed capable of reaching deep into whatever — and whomever — she was looking at.

I'd always known where I stood with her. Back in ninth grade, when I was deep in my rebellious "grownups-are-full-of-it" phase, Claire and I had chosen to assert our independence by sneaking out late at night and wandering around town. We hadn't done much besides wander — Eagle Cove is pretty dull in the middle of the night — but our focus sharpened when we discovered the Double R, the all-night biker bar on the road to Middlemore. The Double R was rough back then (and rough now) and definitely *not* a place for fifteen-year-old girls, but Claire and I became fixated on discovering what went on inside. We planned our infiltration carefully: what we'd wear to appear older, how we'd convince the guy at the door to let us in, how we'd persuade the bartender to let us order drinks, and so on.

We were young and foolish, of course — naive and reckless and stupid — and I shudder at the thought of how things might have gone had events played out differently.

Shortly after midnight on the night of our great adventure, I slipped out of my house and met Claire at the corner, giddy with anticipation. As I prepared to climb into her parents' old pickup — she had the learner's permit, not me — a car quietly rounded the corner and stopped in front of us.

When I saw who was inside, I gasped.

Aunt Emily?

Fear shot through me. *What was she doing here?*

"What is your aunt doing here?" Claire whispered as Emily's headlights splashed over us.

"No idea," I whispered back.

"Find out."

"Me?"

"She's your aunt, not mine."

Heart pounding, I approached her car window.

Emily rolled down the window. "Get in, Sarah," she said, quietly but firmly. "You and Claire both. We have much to discuss."

Shocked that she knew about our plan — how was that even possible? — and terrified that she'd rat us out to our parents, Claire and I did as ordered and slid into her back seat.

Without a word, Emily pulled out and started driving. When we reached the county road, she turned and headed out of town. Through all of this, she didn't speak once. The silence was unnerving — the urge to pipe up and ask what she was doing nearly overwhelming — but somehow Claire and I managed to keep our mouths shut.

When it became clear where we were headed, Claire and I exchanged bewildered glances.

My heart was pounding as Emily pulled into the parking lot of the Double R and slid into a spot at the far end.

She shut off the engine and swiveled to face us. "I don't know if the bouncer will let you in," she said. "I've often wondered."

I could only gape at her, completely flummoxed. "Aunt Emily, what's going on?"

"If he allows you in," Emily continued, "I suggest you consider your next decision carefully." Then, in plain, unadorned language, she laid out in almost clinical detail the various things that bad people sometimes do to teenage girls late at night in biker bars.

"Why are you telling us this?" I said, stunned, barely able to whisper. "Why did you bring us here?"

"You're growing up," she said matter-of-factly. "More and more, the decisions you make will be your own. To make good decisions, you must consider the impact of those decisions. And not just to you."

"What do you mean?"

"I refer to your families, of course. Actions have consequences. If something were to happen to you, I imagine they would be devastated."

Claire spoke up. "You're daring us to go in there."

"Is that what I'm doing?" Emily said mildly.

"You think we don't have the guts."

"Your guts don't worry me. Your judgment does."

I felt my cheeks flame red.

"You're bluffing," Claire said.

"Am I?" Emily replied.

"You'd never let us go in there alone. Not after your big scary speech."

Emily's clear gaze didn't leave Claire's face. "Yet here we are."

I'll always remember the long, tense silence that followed. Two adversaries squaring off, assessing each other, planning their next moves.

I'd already made my decision: I was *never* getting out of that car. But Claire was the braver of us and always had been, and I knew what she was about to do.

Which scared me to death, yet simultaneously made me proud.

My best friend squeezed my arm. "Stay here."

Before I could protest, she pushed open the car door and marched across the parking lot to the entrance of the Double R, high heels crunching in the gravel. As she strode away, I realized she looked like exactly what she was: a gawky teenage girl in her mom's borrowed clothes, wearing too much makeup in hopes of appearing older, and failing miserably. I saw this with a blinding clarity that had eluded me earlier, when the two of us, so full of ourselves, were trying on clothes and testing eyeliner and lipsticks under the mistaken assumption that we knew what we were doing.

"Aunt Emily," I said desperately. "You have to stop her."

"Hush," my aunt said as she rolled down her window. "Not a word. The next moment is key."

Breathless, I watched Claire reach the bouncer. From across the parking lot, I could make out a murmur of conversation but not words. If Claire was following the plan we'd come up with, she was telling the bouncer she wanted to apply for a job. If he asked for ID, she was going to tell him she'd left it at home. If he let her in, she was going to go to the bar to order a vodka cranberry. If the bartender gave her the drink, she was going to pay for it, drink it, and leave — mission accomplished.

(Yes, yes, I know — so dumb!)

The bouncer, a rough-looking bearded guy with tattoos on his neck, was giving Claire the once-over, clearly aware of what he was dealing with and weighing his options. He scanned the parking lot, then asked her something. Her answer seemed to satisfy him. He gestured for her to enter.

For just a second, Claire stood at the door. Then, without any further hesitation, she walked into the Double R.

"Aunt Emily," I blurted out. "We have to get her."

"Quiet, Sarah," she said, then flashed her headlights twice in rapid succession.

At that point, a bunch of stuff happened all at once. Two cars from the sheriff's department roared into the parking lot and four deputies jumped out. Three deputies dashed inside the Double R while the fourth deputy spun the bouncer around and handcuffed him. A minute later, a deputy emerged from the bar holding Claire by her upper arm. Emily flashed her lights again and the deputy brought her to us.

"Get in," Emily said to her.

Claire practically flew into the back seat, shocked and trembling.

Emily said to the deputy, "I assume you have what you need?"

"We got 'em good," he replied.

"I should get the girls home."

"Of course."

"Thank you, Deputy."

"No, ma'am. Thank *you*."

And with that, Emily started the car and pulled out.

"Aunt Emily," I said as the Double R vanished behind us, scarcely able to believe what had just happened. "What in the world…?"

"That, dear, was an intervention."

"An intervention?"

Emily rolled up her window and the roar of the road vanished. In the sudden quiet, she said, "I recently became aware of certain illegal activities involving the owner of the Double R. When your plans came to light, I discussed the matter with the sheriff, and we agreed to leverage the opportunity for mutual benefit."

"Wait," I said, trying to follow. "What?"

"She used us as bait," Claire said, her voice quiet and angry.

"Bait? For what?"

"To go after the Double R," Claire continued. "If they let in minors, they violate their liquor license."

"And?"

"The sheriff can bust them and shut them down."

I allowed her words to sink in, trying to catch up.

"Sarah," Emily added, "the man who owns the Double R is not someone we want doing business in Eagle Cove."

"Claire's right? You used us?"

"Yes." There was neither apology nor celebration in her tone. "It was the best course of action, given the circumstances."

We drove in silence the rest of the ride back to my house, Claire and I too stunned — too scared — to venture any questions.

Emily pulled up next to Claire's pickup. "You girls go home and get some sleep. Come to the cafe tomorrow after school. We'll talk then."

The following afternoon, after a sleepless night and a school day wracked with feverish speculation and fearful anticipation, Claire and I showed up in Emily's cafe as ordered.

My aunt gestured us to a booth in the rear. The day's lunch rush was long over. We had the place mostly to ourselves.

After ringing up a customer, Emily joined us in the booth and finally — and in an odd way, I almost welcomed this — laid into us. With anger and disappointment, she told us, in no uncertain terms, that it was time to shape up and grow up. "We are here to make this world a better place," she said, her all-knowing eyes blazing. "Not worse. Never forget that your decisions, your actions, have consequences. *Always* remember that."

I felt miserable. "Aunt Emily," I said, trying to keep the trembling from my voice. "How much trouble are we in?"

She regarded us for a long moment. "None," she finally said.

Next to me, Claire let out a soft gasp.

"You're not telling our parents?" I said.

"I have no plans to, though I reserve the right to change my mind."

"And the sheriff?"

"He will not require your assistance."

I felt tears coming. "Why are you…?"

Her gaze softened. "Because I love you both, of course."

"But you put us in danger."

"No, dear," she said. "You did that yourselves."

"But," I said, pausing to weigh my words. "You could have stopped us from going there."

"Why would I choose that option?"

"I don't get that."

Claire spoke up. "If she stopped us at the house, we wouldn't have learned our lesson, and the Double R would still be in business."

Emily turned to me. "Sarah, I see you're not convinced."

"I agree we're the ones who put ourselves in danger," I said slowly. "But letting us continue with our plan also put us in danger."

Emily gave me a nod. "There is truth in that. But the larger truth is this: There is risk in every situation and every choice. Safety is an illusion. In terms of how I approached this particular situation,

I weighed the temporary benefit of stopping you against the longer-term benefit of allowing you to participate."

"The longer-term benefit?"

"Your experience last night may prove helpful to you in the future."

I didn't know what to say to that. Next to me, Claire was gazing thoughtfully at my aunt.

"Now," Emily said. "A request." She rose from the booth and returned with a flyer, which she set in front of us.

I stared at it blankly. The flyer was for beginner kung fu classes at Ed's Gym, starting the following week.

"I signed you both up," Emily said.

A jolt went through me. "Why?"

"Because someday, martial arts might come in handy as well."

Emily never told our parents what Claire and I had planned (at least to my knowledge) and I never figured out how she found out. At Ed's Gym, Claire and I got schooled — reluctantly, at first — in kung fu basics, eventually coming around and concluding that martial arts wasn't actually a bad thing to know a bit about. I stopped after the first round of classes (hitting people wasn't my thing, I learned), but Claire kept at it and became a serious student. By the time our senior year rolled around, she was competing in tournaments and doing pretty well, winning more matches than she lost.

I blinked, startled, when I realized I was still staring at the photo of Aunt Emily's chicken feet, lost in thought.

In that moment, I accepted a simple reality: Aunt Emily was fully capable of hiding a dead body in her basement, if she believed she was doing the right thing. She had the nerve, the organizing skills, and a willingness to embrace unorthodox methods.

Still not ready to embrace the conclusion inching toward me, I shook my head. There simply had to be another explanation.

I heard a knock at the door and checked my watch in surprise. Mom wasn't due for another hour. Perhaps it was Janie? Or Gabby or Mr. Benson?

I opened the door and —

For a long second, I couldn't believe what I was seeing.

Standing before me, tall and beautiful and cautiously hopeful, was —

Claire?

CHAPTER 15

"Hey, Sarah," my former best friend said, a tentative smile on her face. "It's been a long time."

Indeed it had. Yet here she was, She Who Shall Not Be Named, here in Eagle Cove, standing before me, in the flesh.

And she looked —

Terrific.

The awkward, coltish, stringy-haired teenager I'd grown up with had transformed into a stunningly elegant swan. Her blond hair was styled in a sleek bob. Her black overcoat, dark jeans, and dark gray wool sweater — all expensive — fit her tall, slim figure perfectly.

She made no attempt to hug me. Her manner radiated awareness and caution. Clearly she understood her arrival would be a surprise, and not a wholly welcome one.

"Claire," I finally said. "What are you doing here?"

"I almost called," she said apologetically, "but I thought it would be better to come in person."

"In person?" I repeated.

"My company's been hired for a short consulting gig at Middlemore University. I start tomorrow."

"Middlemore?" I said, apparently unable to stop repeating her.

"For the next two weeks," she said. "When the assignment came up, I jumped at it. It seemed like a good time to come back and check in on everyone."

I realized I was being rude. "Please, come in."

"Thank you." She stepped past me into the living room, then turned to face me. "Sarah, I'm so sorry about Aunt Emily."

"Thank you," I said, blinking back a rush of emotion.

"She meant more to me than I can express," she said, starting to tear up. "I was in Singapore when I heard the news, on another project. Otherwise I would have been here for the funeral."

"I appreciate that. No worries."

There was an awkward pause. "How are your mom and Grace?"

"Grace is fine. She's still working at Middlemore, so you can see while you're there. Mom is holding up."

Claire nodded sympathetically. "She and Emily were very close."

"Best friends."

Claire blinked at the words and shifted her gaze to the photo wall. "It must be very hard for her."

"She didn't get out of bed for three days. But yesterday she went back to work."

"Keeping busy can help."

"It can. But you know how grief goes. It's a day-by-day thing."

"Is she still working for the town?"

"For the mayor."

A short buzz interrupted us. Claire pulled her phone out of her jacket and glanced at it with a frown.

"Sorry," she said. "Work thing."

"If you need to talk to your colleagues…."

"It can wait." She slipped the phone back into her pocket. "Though I do have to get back to Middlemore."

"I see," I said, though I really didn't.

She compressed her lips — something she did when making a decision. "I drove here because I wanted to ask two questions."

I felt myself tensing. "Ask away."

"First, can we have dinner? Not tonight, but in a night or two?" After a nervous breath, she continued. "Maybe you and me and Janie? I would love to catch up. It's been too long — totally my fault — and I want us to … reconnect."

Not until I yell and scream at you and chew you out for abandoning us, I didn't say.

"Of course," I said, relieved to hear my voice sounding calm. "I'm here for the next ten days."

"Great," she said, with an emotion that I interpreted as relief.

"And your second question?"

"Before I ask," she said. "I just want to say, if it's not possible or convenient, please say no."

"Okay…."

Claire squared her shoulders. "I'm hoping I can crash in the studio apartment downstairs while I'm here."

I blinked with surprise. "You want to stay *here?*"

"Only if it's okay."

"Middlemore's thirty minutes away. Why not a hotel there?"

"I don't mind the drive." She took a deep breath. "And honestly, the main reason I took the project was to spend time in Eagle Cove. I'd hoped I could stay at the farm, but Mom and Dad have tourists coming this weekend, so that's out. Then I remembered Emily's studio and how she sometimes let people stay in it and I thought, staying here would mean more time to catch up with everyone...."

She trailed off, waiting for me to respond.

As the silence lengthened, I realized I needed to give her an answer. Which meant I needed to figure out how I felt about her staying here. If I was okay with that, why wasn't I already saying so? If I wasn't, then what was my issue?

"Sure," I finally said, though I wasn't sure at all. "That won't be a problem."

"Great. Thank you. I really appreciate it." Her phone buzzed again and she grimaced, then shot me a regretful look. "Sorry, have to go. I have a room in Middlemore tonight, but I'll be back tomorrow."

In the entry foyer, I took a pair of keys from the sideboard drawer. "For the hallway door downstairs," I said, handing her the keys, "and the studio."

She stared at me for a moment, then pulled me in for a hug. "Thank you," she whispered in my ear. "Can't wait to catch up." Her shampoo, or maybe her perfume, smelled faintly of jasmine. She released me before I could return the hug. "See you tomorrow?"

"See you tomorrow," I said as I opened the door.

With a smile, she headed out.

I listened to her footsteps on the stairs and then closed the door firmly, my mind and heart awhirl with sudden urgent questions, the past and present colliding in ways I'd never expected.

CHAPTER 16

The next morning, I found myself on my hands and knees in the cafe, scrubbing away at a stubborn grease stain on the floor near the cash register, wishing a certain former best friend had picked a different moment to show up at my door. I'd barely slept the previous night, tossing and turning as everything that had been thrown at me — the divorce, the layoff, Anna starting college, Emily's death, the body in the basement, the cafe's imminent reopening, Claire's sudden reappearance — threatened to overwhelm me.

No, that wasn't right. Things were way past threat stage: I was officially, totally, undeniably overwhelmed.

I scrubbed harder. Though my life was a mess, no way was this tenacious stain going to beat me.

The day, not even half over, had already been a

busy one. Barney, the town's building inspector, had shown up first thing. After reviewing our to-do lists and telling us which tasks were essential, he'd helped me and Janie hook up the gas to the ovens and given us the okay to start baking.

After he left, I'd told Janie about Claire's surprise appearance. Shocked but pleased, Janie announced plans to make a carrot cake — Claire's favorite — to celebrate. From the kitchen, I heard her moving around, humming a song to herself.

In that moment, I wished I could be more like Janie. I wished I could dwell less on life's past disappointments and focus more on what was good in the here and now. Maybe if I got better at rolling, I wouldn't feel so stuck.

The cafe door opened and a gust of crisp autumn air rushed in.

"Morning," a voice said. I glanced up and found a stocky man in his mid-forties with thinning gray hair and a jowly face, dressed in a mailman's uniform, a bag bulging with letters slung over his shoulder. "Delivery for Sarah Boone."

"That's me," I said, reaching for a rag to wipe off my hands.

"So you're Nancy's daughter," he said as he set the heavy mailbag down with a grunt.

"That's right," I said, getting to my feet. "And you are?"

"Eddie Jones, your mailman." He pulled a letter

out of his bag. "I have a registered letter for Sarah Boone."

"Then you've come to the right place."

"I'll need to see ID."

My eyebrows rose. Apparently, this Eddie fellow was the conscientious type. I grabbed my handbag, rooted through it for my wallet, then held out my driver's license for him to read.

He examined the ID and then me. "California?"

"That's where I live now."

"Heard you grew up here."

"That's right."

"Need you to sign."

"Sure."

He held out a piece of paper and offered me a pen, which I used to scrawl my signature.

"Heard you're opening the cafe again," he said, his gaze roving over the space.

"Just for the festival," I said.

"Heard about the dead fellow you found, too."

"Yes," I said, not sure what else to say.

"Heard he had it coming."

"Is that so?" I said, going on alert. "In what way?"

"Going after his wife like that," he said, his tone full of disapproval.

My pulse quickened — the town and I

appeared to be thinking along the same lines. "You ever run into him?"

For a split second, surprise crossed his face. "Him? No, I don't think so." He checked his watch. "I should get going. The mail doesn't deliver itself." He hoisted the mailbag onto his shoulder. "Good luck with opening day."

"Good meeting you, Eddie. See you soon." I watched him leave, unsure about what had just happened. Had I seen a flash of concern when I asked if he'd met the dead man? Or was my overactive imagination going too far?

I turned my attention to the manila envelope in my hands. The envelope had been postmarked yesterday. I frowned at the return address. Why would Jim Atkins, my aunt's lawyer, send me a registered letter via the postal service? His office was two blocks away. Why not walk the letter over, or call and have me swing by?

I opened the manila envelope. Inside was a sealed letter-size envelope with five words written on it:

For Sarah, with my apologies.

I gasped — the handwriting was unmistakably Aunt Emily's.

With shaking hands, I tore open the envelope, pulled out a letter, and read:

My dearest Sarah,

I deeply regret that circumstances require this communication.

I left instructions with my lawyer to deliver this letter to you after my death in the event that a man's body is discovered in the basement of my building. A similar letter has been sent to the sheriff.

I alone am responsible for this man's death. He broke into the building and attacked me. To defend myself, I shot him with a nail gun. I dried out the body to prevent discovery and took steps to hinder identification of the remains. Then I hid the body.

I did all of this without the help of anyone, including my tenants. I want to be very clear on this point. Gabby McBride, Donald Benson, and Amy Messina were not involved in, and had no knowledge of, the death or burial of this man.

I am at peace with my actions. The man threatened me with violence. A woman has a right to defend herself. I exercised that right.

What happened is as plain and simple as that.

My only regret is that you must now sort through the consequences of my actions.

With love, gratitude and respect,
Emily

I found my way to a chair and sat down, shaking with emotions I could barely keep in check.

Aunt Emily had killed the man in the basement?

I couldn't believe it — it seemed impossible. Yet

the letter in my hand said otherwise. The handwriting was hers. The words, clear and forthright, sounded just like her.

Still, the thought came: Maybe the letter wasn't real. Maybe it was a hoax. A prank.

Only one way to find out.

I grabbed my phone and called Jim Atkins, my aunt's lawyer.

He picked up on the second ring. "Good morning, Sarah. I've been expecting your call."

"Jim, I...." I stared at the letter in front of me, at a loss where to begin. "What in the world is this about?"

"That depends."

I frowned. "What do you mean?"

"Your aunt instructed me to send the letters, but she didn't reveal what was in them."

"You mean you don't know what the letters say?" I said, flabbergasted.

"No, I don't. The envelopes were sealed." He paused. "I will share, however, that I had grave reservations about your aunt's instructions, since they suggested she had knowledge of a crime."

"How did she persuade you to go along?"

"She assured me she had no such knowledge."

I swallowed back a wave of emotion as I absorbed what he was saying.

"And you believed her?"

"She insisted no crime had occurred. She also

refused to share any additional information. It put me in a difficult position."

"But in the end…."

"In the end, because she was my client and my friend, and because she insisted that nothing criminal had occurred, I reluctantly agreed to honor her wishes."

I swallowed again. "Even though you didn't believe her."

For a long moment, he remained silent. Then I heard him sigh. "Sarah — and I say this to you in confidence — my assumption from the start was that Emily was lying."

"Well, you weren't wrong. Do you want to know what the letter says?"

"Very much so."

"She says she killed the guy in the basement. Self-defense."

"I feared as much. Did she also state she did it alone?"

"Yes."

He sighed again. "Very well. Would you mind sharing the letter with me?"

"Not at all. I'll send you a photo."

"Thank you."

In the background over the phone, I heard a noise. Then Jim said, "I'm sorry, the sheriff is here. Can I call you later?"

"Of course."

The line dropped. I sat silent and motionless, staring at the letter, the afternoon sun warming the booth, allowing my great-aunt's revelations to sink in.

Janie emerged from the kitchen. "Cake's in the oven," she said. "I'm also making cookies and I need a taste tester. I'll leave a plate on the counter."

"Great," I said absently, still lost in shock.

Her brow furrowed. "Something up?" When I didn't reply, she gestured to the letter. "What's that?"

"Oh, nothing," I said, not ready to share. "Just thinking about Aunt Emily."

"Oh," she said sympathetically.

I stood up. "Is it okay if I run upstairs for a bit?"

"Of course. I'll be heading to the grocery store — we need vanilla — but won't be gone long. Come down when you're ready."

"Thanks," I said with a grateful smile.

A minute later, in my aunt's apartment and comfortably ensconced in her rocking chair, I reread the letter, then reread it again.

Finally, with a grunt of disappointment, I gave up and leaned back. I needed to think clearly about this, something my brain hadn't been very good at lately.

Step up, Sarah. Aunt Emily would expect nothing less.

The gentle back-and-forth motion of the rocker comforted me as my mind floated, my gaze wandering over Emily's wall of travel photos. For several moments, random thoughts and emotions flowed unfiltered.

Until I realized: At least some of the answers were here for the taking, one floor below.

If I could pry them loose.

I stood up and returned to the cafe. A batch of Janie's chocolate-chip cookies, fresh from the oven and smelling divine, lay on a plate on the counter. I grabbed the plate and made my way up to the second floor, where I knocked on Mr. Benson's door.

When he opened the door, I held out the plate.

"Thank you," I said.

Mr. Benson stared at the cookies, puzzled. "Thank me? For what?"

"For being a true friend to Aunt Emily. For helping her in her hour of need."

After a pause, he straightened his posture. "Emily was a remarkable woman. She showed me many kindnesses over the years." He glanced again at the cookies. "What do you know?"

With my other hand, I took the letter from my back pocket and held it up. "I know she had help."

He exhaled, held the door open, and stood aside. "You best come in. I'm sure you have questions."

CHAPTER 17

From the building's architectural plans, I knew that Mr. Benson had a one-bath, one-bedroom apartment, but I hadn't been inside yet. I looked around the open living-dining area with interest. The room had a decidedly scholarly air, with floor-to-ceiling shelves lining the walls crammed with books. On the dining table, two stacks — one of books, one of papers — rested near an open laptop and a cup of tea. Near the windows, a worn leather sofa and wingback side chair faced a TV, one of those bulky old-style models built with vacuum tubes. The room smelled faintly of old books— hardly surprising — but otherwise seemed orderly and clean.

Mr. Benson set the plate of cookies on the dining table, then stepped into the galley kitchen and leaned into what I realized was the open dumbwaiter door.

"Gabby, you there?" he yelled into it. "You'll want to come over."

"Right now?" I heard her yell back.

"Yes, woman, right now!"

I gaped at him. "You and Gabby share the dumbwaiter?"

"That's how the building was set up."

"And you talk with each other through it?"

"Easier than the phone."

"Why did you invite her over?"

He blinked, surprised. "Why wouldn't I?"

"You don't like each other."

"Who ever said that?"

"But … you're always yelling at each other."

He waved the objection away. "Who doesn't do that?"

"But….

"Young lady, Gabby McBride is one of my dearest friends."

"But she annoys you so much!"

"Who doesn't get annoyed from time to time?"

The apartment door opened and Gabby shuffled in. "What's up, old crank?" She stiffened when she saw me. "What are *you* doing here?"

Mr. Benson said, "Gabby, she knows."

Gabby's eyes narrowed. "Nonsense."

"She knows."

Gabby shook her head with disgust. "Well, fudgepockets." She made her way to the couch and settled into what I guessed was her usual spot. "Couldn't keep your big piehole shut, could you?"

"Piehole?" Mr. Benson repeated, stunned. "*Pie*hole?"

"It's what the kids are saying these days," Gabby said. "Or maybe it's *cake*hole? Not that you'd know, you old stick-in-the-mud."

"Gabby," I said, "Mr. Benson didn't tell me."

"Then who did?"

"No one." I held my aunt's letter in front of me. "Including Aunt Emily."

Mr. Benson said, "What is that?"

"A letter from her. Delivered a few minutes ago. If you'd like, I can read it."

Mr. Benson settled onto the sofa next to Gabby and gestured me to the wingback side chair. The two of them listened as I read the letter aloud. Hearing my aunt's words seemed to bring her back to life, her strong presence filling the room.

When I finished, Mr. Benson glanced at Gabby, who returned his gaze, exhaling mightily.

I heard a faint scratching sound in the kitchen and saw Mr. Snuggles emerge from the dumbwaiter shaft. With skillful confidence, he leaped to the floor and made his way into the living room, where he jumped up and settled down between Gabby and Mr. Benson.

Now I had three pairs of eyes staring at me.

Mr. Benson broke the silence. "Young lady, we're willing to tell you what happened. But only if you promise discretion."

"No yapping to your sheriff boyfriend," Gabby added.

I sighed. "He's not my boyfriend."

"Ha," Gabby said. "Just a matter of time."

"Gabby," Mr. Benson said, "let the poor girl be."

"Destiny, the two of you," Gabby said. "Ever since high school, mooning over each other. The only real question is, what are you waiting for?"

I started to open my mouth, but no words came out. Because what could I say?

Gabby was clearly disappointed. "Too scared — is that it?"

"Gabby," Mr. Benson said again, exasperated.

She leaned forward. "That louse of a husband did a number on you, didn't he?"

"Gabby!"

"Fine," Gabby said. "Go ahead, ignore me like you always do."

"Only way to stay sane," Mr. Benson shot back.

Gabby sniffed. "What's that I smell?"

"A plate of Janie's cookies, fresh from the oven," I said. "As a thank you."

She glared at me, offended. "You brought cookies for *him*, but not me?"

"Your plate is coming. Before I realized you two were so … friendly, I thought I'd have to tackle you individually, and that Mr. Benson would be…."

"Easier?" Gabby prompted.

"Well…."

"Softer? More gullible? More prone to persuasion?"

"Shut your piehole, woman," Mr. Benson said.

"Ha!" Gabby said triumphantly. "See? I'll drag you into this century yet."

"Woman, I —"

Gabby cut him off with a short laugh, then turned toward me. "Fooled you, didn't we?"

"Fooled me?"

"Me and ye old crank here."

"Oh, about you two being bitter enemies."

She cackled again.

"You missed your calling," I said.

"The stage? The silver screen?" She straightened her back and extended an arm skyward, the pose dramatic and unexpectedly graceful. In that second, I caught a glimpse of her as she'd once been — the same irrepressible spirit in a youthful, limber body.

Mr. Benson cleared his throat. "Sarah, we'd prefer you keep what we share between us."

I considered that for a moment. "How about this: I won't say a thing unless I need to help somebody who's in trouble."

Mr. Benson shifted his gaze to Gabby, who gave him a nod. "Very well," he said. "As the sheriff indicated, Peter Messina is the man in the basement. He was married to Amy Messina. We met Amy when she showed up here one day, bruised and bleeding."

"Courtesy of Peter the wife beater," Gabby added darkly.

"Amy showed up here? On the run from her husband?"

"Yes," Mr. Benson said.

"Why here?"

"Emily had known Amy's parents. So when Amy showed up here, of course Emily took her in."

"Poor thing was terrified," Gabby said. "At her wit's end."

"Amy had tried to leave her husband before, but Peter had tracked her down and coerced her into going back to him. He was from a family known for violence and vengeance."

I swallowed, appalled at what I was hearing. "Emily told you all this?"

"She had to tell us," Mr. Benson said. "We saw Amy's bruises. Also, she needed to alert us to the danger, in case we ran into him."

I almost didn't want to ask, but I forged ahead. "How did Peter die?"

Mr. Benson and Gabby exchanged another glance.

"Sure you want to know?" Gabby said.

I wasn't sure at all, but at the same time I knew I simply had no choice. "Yes."

"Emily killed him," Gabby said. "Shot him with a nail gun. Right in his cold black heart."

I couldn't restrain a gasp. So it really was true — it had happened just as Emily had written. "Were you there?"

Mr. Benson shook his head. "She told us what happened when we helped her move the body."

I gasped again. "You moved it? From where?"

"From the basement to the storeroom."

"We stuffed him in the food dehydrator," Gabby said, almost proudly. "To dry him out."

I shook my head, trying to picture the scene. "Emily and Peter were in the basement when it happened? Why?"

"He chased Emily there. He was trying to force her to tell him where Amy was."

"And she…."

"She grabbed the nail gun and shot him when he attacked her."

"How did you get involved?"

Gabby gestured toward the kitchen, and I realized she was pointing to the dumbwaiter. "I heard her cry out."

"The sound carried up from the basement?"

"Clear as a bell," Gabby said.

"We knew we needed to investigate," Mr. Benson said. "So we went down and…."

"You found them," I said, shaking my head, trying to absorb everything they'd just revealed.

"You need a cookie," Mr. Benson said. He rose from the couch and retrieved Janie's plate. "Take one, young lady," he ordered, holding the plate in front of me.

"A big bite," Gabby said.

I did as ordered and bit in, amazed as always at how wonderful Janie's cookies tasted. The rich chocolate chunks, still warm, melted in my mouth.

"We kept the body in the dehydrator for two months," Gabby said. "Got it nice and leathery."

"And then?"

"We moved it to the basement and built a wall to hide it."

"The three of you?" I asked.

"Yes," Mr. Benson said. "Amy knew what happened, but she wasn't involved in Peter's death or hiding the body."

"How did she react when she found out?"

"We don't know," Mr. Benson said. "The truth is, we barely met her. A few brief encounters in the hallway, no conversation. She always seemed very frightened."

"Scared little rabbit," Gabby said. "Mousy, brown hair over her face, shoulders hunched, rushing to hide away in the studio."

The picture they painted was vivid and heartbreaking. "Poor thing," I said. "What happened to her?"

"No idea," Gabby said. "The morning after Peter died, she was gone."

"With Emily's help?"

Mr. Benson said, "Emily told us she helped Amy start a new life."

"A new life?" I said. "Meaning what?"

"We have no idea. We don't know the details. We agreed it was better that way."

"In case we got grilled by nosy parkers like you," Gabby said.

"And you haven't seen her since?"

"Not even once."

As I took in these two people, I realized I was truly seeing them for the first time. Mr. Benson — with his sweater vests, wire-rimmed glasses, and air of cautious reserve — seemed the epitome of conventional respectability. But when his friend had needed him, he'd demonstrated loyalty, courage, and a willingness to ignore the law. And Gabby, an impatient, sharp-tongued busybody if there ever was one, had displayed a fiercely protective instinct that warmed my heart.

"Why did you two agree to help Emily?" I said. "You were taking such a huge risk."

"Your aunt needed us," Mr. Benson said. "For me, it was as simple as that."

"Darn tootin'," Gabby said.

I felt myself tear up. "She was lucky to have you in her life."

To my surprise, Gabby teared up as well. "Friends first — that's my motto," she said gruffly.

"Even when they break the law?"

"Bah," she said with a wave. "Rules are for weenies."

Mr. Benson sighed. "I would use different words, but I agree with the sentiment." He sat up straighter, his gaze intensifying. "Friends and family are what matter most in this life. Value them. Treasure them."

"Break the rules for them?"

"When necessary? Absolutely."

CHAPTER 18

At that moment, we heard footsteps on the stairs in the hallway, followed by the faint sound of the studio apartment door opening and shutting.

"Who's that?" Gabby said, sitting up straighter.

"That's Claire," I said.

Gabby's gaze sharpened. "Your friend Claire?"

"The one and only."

"What's she doing in Eagle Cove?"

Briefly, I shared the previous night's conversation.

Gabby shook her head. "I don't like it."

"What's not to like?" Mr. Benson said, his brow furrowing.

"The coincidence."

"Coincidence?"

"Sarah unearths Peter the wife beater in the

basement. The very next day, Claire shows up and moves in."

"Wait," I said, not following. "What does one have to do with the other?"

"Claire doesn't bother coming to Emily's funeral, but as soon as a body is discovered, she's here?"

I shook my head, unable to see a connection. "She was in Singapore on a consulting project."

"Singapore's halfway around the world," Mr. Benson added.

Gabby snorted. "I know where Singapore is, you old crank."

"Then what in tarnation are you going on about, woman?"

"Something's not right." She got to her feet and slowly straightened her back. "No matter what you nimrods think."

I bit my lip, struggling to keep my expression neutral. "She'll be here for two weeks. I'll make sure she swings by to say hi."

Gabby shook her head, disappointed. "Sometimes you almost seem smart. And then...." She shuffled to the door. "Just remember, keep your trap shut. This conversation never happened."

After the door closed behind her, Mr. Benson said apologetically, "She doesn't really think we're nimrods."

I smiled. "I'm pretty sure she does. Which is

fine." I rose from the chair. "I should get going. Lots to do downstairs."

Mr. Benson stood with me. "I hope all of this doesn't change how you feel about your aunt."

"It definitely expands my understanding of her."

"Uncovering the past can be a troublesome business. But please know that what Emily did, she did for the right reasons."

"I appreciate you saying that," I said, swallowing back a rush of feeling.

He gestured to the cookie plate. "Will Janie be making these during the festival?"

I smiled. "Should she?"

He picked one up and bit in. "Mmm, most definitely."

"I'll tell her you approve."

In the hallway, I paused briefly in front of the studio apartment, debating whether to knock on the door. But I decided to give Claire time to settle in and I continued downstairs. As I stepped through the cafe's hallway door, my phone buzzed. I pulled it out of my pocket.

My heart rate picked up when I saw who it was.

"Hey, Matt," I said.

"Hey, Sarah." His voice was low and rumbly. "Bet you know why I'm calling."

"Quite a letter, isn't it?"

"I'd like to see yours, if you don't mind."

"Of course. We still on for coffee later?"

"About that," he said apologetically. "I'll be tied up this afternoon, thanks to your aunt. Can we reschedule?"

"Of course," I said, ignoring the stab of disappointment. "How about I send you a photo of the letter? I'll leave the actual letter in the cafe and you can swing by whenever."

"Thanks, I appreciate it."

"By the way, guess who's back in town?"

He paused. "Who?"

"Claire."

"Claire? Wow."

"She showed up last night. She'll be here for a couple of weeks."

"What brings her here?"

"Her consulting firm has a project at Middlemore."

"Tell her I look forward to seeing her."

"Will do. And hey, can I switch topics? I have a question about Peter Messina."

"Sure," he said, though I sensed him becoming guarded.

"Was he a bad guy?"

He sighed. "Is that the word around town?"

"Seems so."

"I can tell you this. Peter Messina had an arrest for domestic disturbance, though the charges were eventually dropped. A few months after that, Amy Messina filed a restraining order against him."

"You know anything more about her?"

"Not yet. We're not even sure where she is now."

"Matt," I said, trying to figure out how to say what I wanted to say without giving away too much. "Do you believe what Aunt Emily wrote in her letter?"

"It's not about what I believe. It's about what the evidence shows."

I considered his words. "So if you're going only by the evidence — if that's the only standard — then the mystery of the man in the basement appears to be solved."

He sighed. "I promised I'd keep you in the loop, Sarah, and I'll continue to do so."

"Which I appreciate."

"What the letter says might be difficult to accept. But I'd like you to hold off digging further, at least for now, at least until we know more."

I already know more, I didn't say.

His tone sharpened. "Unless you already know more."

"What?" I said, taken aback. Had he already guessed I'd coaxed the truth out of Gabby and Mr. Benson? Was he secretly telepathic? "What would I know?"

He didn't reply — he didn't have to. He knew that I knew exactly what he was thinking.

"Matt," I said, mentally crossing my fingers, "If I hear anything that might prove helpful, I'll let you know."

"You," he said with a sigh, "can be very exasperating."

"Oh, come on," I said, trying to inject a playful note. "You don't really mean that."

"Yes," he said. "I do."

I didn't know what to say to that and apparently neither did he, because the silence that followed became rather awkward.

Finally, he said, "Sarah, I just want you to be safe."

"I appreciate that. I will be, I promise."

"I'll call you about coffee?"

"Sounds good."

"Talk to you soon."

And he was gone. I glanced around the cafe. The kitchen was silent. Janie hadn't come back yet from the store.

I made my way to a table near the front window and settled into a chair, trying to understand why I didn't feel more upset about the day's revelations. My beloved aunt had just reached out from the grave and confessed to killing someone. In a terrible moment that must have haunted her afterward, she'd found herself threatened with harm and been forced to resort to drastic measures to save herself.

Why wasn't I beside myself with concern and sadness and outrage?

Because it didn't happen like that, my inner voice said.

I sat upright, shocked, as the thought rocketed through me.

My heart started beating faster. What nonsense, I told myself, pushing back. She admitted doing it. Two witnesses support her story.

To which my inner voice replied:

She lied.

A laugh burst forth, sharp and loud, surprising me with its force. What an absurd idea!

Let the truth percolate, my inner voice continued, undaunted. *You'll come around in time.*

I grunted with frustration. Sometimes my inner voice could be extremely annoying — smug and insufferable, an annoying know-it-all. It never seemed to appreciate that truth had a time and a place. It never seemed to care that sometimes, truth was the last thing I wanted to hear.

I became aware of the letter in my jeans pocket, pressing against my thigh. The words my aunt had written on that piece of paper were either the truth or they weren't. Regardless, now was not the time to find out. There was simply too much to do. For now, I was going to go along with Emily's explanation: She'd acted in self-defense.

My gaze fell to the floor in front of the cash register, and to the grease stain that was still painfully visible. With a quiet groan, I dropped from the chair onto my hands and knees, grabbed my sponge, and resumed scrubbing.

CHAPTER 19

The next week proved a relentless, never-ending slog — a battle between necessary tasks and limited energy, with exhaustion quickly gaining the upper hand. Janie and I worked from dawn to dusk, trying desperately to get everything ready in time for the festival, scrubbing and mopping and hammering and painting and tossing and organizing up a storm. The days blurred together. Each morning, I awakened in my childhood bedroom, muscles tired and sore and crying for relief, and greeted the day by cursing Mayor Johnson with unrestrained gusto. Then I hauled myself upright, staggered into the shower, creakily slipped into clothes, and drove myself back to the new epicenter of my universe of pain.

Janie quickly figured out a morning routine to jumpstart me out of my morning funk. While I sat at a table like a lump, bleary-eyed and sullen, staring resentfully at the endless list of tasks yelling at me from my laptop screen, Janie (bless her!) would set a fresh blueberry scone and hot latte on the table and slide into the chair opposite me.

After she watched me take a bite and a sip, a smile would appear on her kind face and she'd say, "Ready for a new day, Miss Grumpyface?"

Invariably, the words would provoke a grin and, fortified by life-saving doses of sugar and caffeine, I'd shoo my inner whiner to the side and begin the difficult process of becoming human again.

"I don't deserve you," I'd say.

"Right back atcha," she'd say with a smile.

And after giving my shoulders a stretch, I'd sit up straighter and hear myself say, "Okay, what's next?"

Three nights after Claire showed up, Janie and I had dinner with her across the street at Mario's. She told us about her project at Middlemore — something boring and technical about upgrading the university's data center — and caught us up on her post-divorce life. She was dating occasionally, but there was no one serious, and she was spending too much time at work. When she apologized for being a bad communicator, Janie and I made the expected understanding noises.

On the surface, the dinner had gone well. It had been good seeing Claire again and having the three of us in the same room. But as enjoyable as the evening was, something had felt off.

That something was me. Because I'd held back. Even with two glasses of Cabernet sloshing through my veins, I'd failed to work up the courage to do what I wanted — no, *needed* — to do.

I hadn't called my former best friend on the carpet.

I hadn't laid into her about ditching me and abandoning our friendship.

And I hadn't found out why she'd done it.

If the past two years had taught me anything, it was that I was no longer capable of papering over stuff that mattered. I was no longer able to ignore or avoid or deflect the way I had before. Try as I might, it was getting harder for me to pretend.

A reckoning with Claire was imminent, though I didn't have time to dwell on that now. Throughout the week, as Janie and I pushed through our tasks, the cafe received a steady stream of visitors. Eagle Cove was an inquisitive town, and between the corpse in the basement and the cafe being reopened, a lot of curious folks stopped by. Mayor Johnson checked in daily on our progress. Jerry Meachum, true to his word, pitched in to help with heavy lifting and painting. Gabby and Mr. Benson and Mr. Snuggles made frequent appearances. Gabby introduced me to "the girls," a trio of octogenarians who apparently traveled as a flock and preferred to be addressed as Mrs. Bunch, Mrs. Chan, and Ms. Hollingsworth. "Me and the girls, we'll be playing bridge here," Gabby informed me, pointing to the booth nearest the door. "Best seats in the house."

I also met the *Gazette*'s new reporter, Wendy Danvers. A few years younger and a few pounds slimmer than me, with a pleasant face and shoulder-length brown hair, she came across as energetic and upbeat. When I mentioned I'd interned at the paper, she gave me a knowing smile. "So you know Bob." When I told her I appreciated Bob's unusual take on current events, she added, "Glad to hear. I hope that means you'll get a laugh out of tomorrow's edition."

"What do you mean?"

"He thinks the guy you found in your basement, Peter Messina, was tied to a conspiracy of some sort."

My eyebrows rose. "What kind of conspiracy?"

"He's not sure, and it's driving him crazy." She sighed. "I mean, what happened seems pretty cut-and-dried to me."

"What do you think happened?" I said cautiously.

"We won't be publishing this, because we have no proof. But my take is that Amy Messina killed her abusive husband and your aunt helped her cover it up."

I couldn't disagree — I suspected the same — but my thoughts immediately went to Mom. If the *Gazette* were ever to publish an article alleging Emily's involvement in a murder or a coverup, Mom would be very upset.

My face must have telegraphed something, because I saw Wendy's expression sharpen. "What don't I know?"

"Nothing," I lied immediately. "Matt — the sheriff, I mean — hasn't shared much yet."

She looked at me shrewdly. "The two of you grew up here."

"That's right."

"You go way back."

"That's right."

"If you asked him, he'd probably tell you."

"Oh, I doubt that," I said, trying to act like the very idea made me uncomfortable.

Her gaze became even more knowing. "I bet he'd tell you whatever you wanted."

She's met him, I realized.

More than that: *She knows we dated.*

A light bulb went off. It wasn't just the body in the basement that interested Wendy.

She's attracted to Matt — and wants to know if I'm competition.

I glanced at her left hand. *No wedding ring.* My cheeks flamed pink. "It's probably best to leave the investigating to the professionals."

"Aren't you interested? Even a bit?"

"Sure," I said, trying to act like we were still talking about the dead man. "But honestly, right now…." I waved my arm around. "I'm so busy, I barely have time to sleep."

She seemed to accept the truth of that as she eyed a freshly painted stretch of wall. "I should let you get back to it."

"Thank you, but please stop by whenever. Janie and I will be here, plugging away, trying to get everything ready for the festival."

At that moment, the ring of the cafe doorbell heralded a new arrival. The woman who stepped inside was — how to put this — *not from here*. Slim and petite, around my age and height, she had thick, lustrous red hair that tumbled onto her shoulders. Beneath a creamy wool shawl she wore a long-sleeved silk dress — midnight-blue, like a gown from another era — that fit snugly around her waist and flowed dramatically to the floor. Her makeup was on the heavy side, but expertly, beautifully applied.

She closed the door behind her and said, with a lush Southern accent, "I'm so sorry to intrude." Her voice was low and musical; I could feel it drawing me in.

I cleared my throat. "Good afternoon. Is there something I can help you with?"

"Oh, I do hope so." Her expressive green eyes

turned to me. "Allow me to introduce myself. My name is Hialeah Truegood."

"Sarah Boone," I said, extending my hand.

She took my hand in both of hers, her touch light, her fingers cool. "I'm a visitor to your beautiful town, here from New Orleans."

"Oh, I love New Orleans," I replied.

"As do I. New Orleans is my heart and soul. It's where I was born and where I will die."

It seemed an oddly confident statement. "What brings you to Eagle Cove?"

She fixed me with a warm smile. "I felt a call to come north and experience the beauty of autumn in New England."

"You've come to the right place."

"A man at the inn mentioned the Harvest Festival," she said, her gaze roving, "and this cafe reopening."

"That's right. Just a few days away."

"Are you the owner?"

"I am."

Her gaze lingered on a table near the window, then returned to me. "I realize that what I'm about to share, and ask, may seem unusual."

"Please, go ahead."

"I'm a medium," she said simply. "I have the gift of communicating with departed spirits."

"Is that so?" I said, willing myself to keep my

face still. I'd never believed in that kind of thing and doubted I ever would.

"The moment I saw this lovely space, I felt drawn to it." Again, her attention returned to the small table near the window. "There is an energy here that would be most beneficial for my readings."

"Your readings?"

"My life's calling," she said solemnly. "So many people need the guidance that only their departed loved ones can provide."

I realized what she was asking. "You're wondering if it would be okay to do readings here."

"Yes, Ms. Boone, I am. How wonderful if that would be possible." She reached out and again took hold of my hand. "To be able to offer support and comfort to so many."

I tried to sort out the jumble of thoughts and feelings running through me. My immediate instinct was to say no. If what I'd always suspected about psychics was true, then this woman was either deluded or a scammer.

But other thoughts rushed in, demanding to be heard. Wasn't it possible I was being harsh and unfair? I'd been wrong about so many things in my life, after all — who was I declare that psychic communication wasn't possible? And regardless, if a person found comfort and solace from a reading, what was wrong with that?

My business side clicked on. *What if these readings could bring in new customers?*

"Do readings make folks hungry or thirsty?" I asked.

"Oh, yes," she said immediately. "The experience can be very intense. I always recommend a hot beverage and food."

I realized Wendy Danvers had been standing there the whole time, listening with interest. After apologizing for my rudeness, I made introductions. While the two of them chatted, I spied Janie at the kitchen doorway, her hands coated in flour. She'd heard as well, apparently.

I cocked my head, silently asking what she thought, and she shrugged, telling me she was fine with it.

I turned to our visitor. "Ms. Truegood, how about we take it day-to-day and see how it goes?"

"Oh, thank you," she said with a warm smile. "Thank you so much. And please, call me Hialeah. I have such a positive feeling about this. We can do so much good here. I promise you won't regret it."

CHAPTER 20

Two days before the Harvest Festival started, Janie and I reached a rather stunning conclusion:

We were ready for business!

A week of hard work had transformed a dusty, neglected space back into a bright, cheery cafe. The stacks of boxes were gone — banished to the basement, which Matt had given us permission to enter again. The walls, formerly dirty and faded, sported a fresh coat of white paint. The cafe's red vinyl booths and chrome tables and chairs had been scrubbed and buffed to gleaming perfection. The ovens and refrigerators and other appliances were clean and ready to go. The display counter was stuffed with plates of freshly baked muffins, scones, and cookies — all due to Janie, whose baking mastery knew no bounds. On the floor in front of the cash register, a certain troublesome stain had finally disappeared. When Barney had swung by that morning for his final inspection, he'd looked around appreciatively and given us his okay.

"Let's open early," I heard myself say.

Janie gave me a smile. "A test run?"

"A soft opening. Tomorrow morning. We can work out the kinks before the crowds arrive."

"Great idea." She pointed to my laptop. "You sure we've gotten to everything on our must-do list?"

"I think so," I said, scanning the spreadsheet.

"Maybe we should start on our 'if-we-have-time' tasks."

"You really are a glutton for punishment." I flipped to our secondary task list and swung the laptop toward her so she could see the list as well.

"There is one thing I'd like to start on," I said after a minute.

"What's that?"

"I'd love to close that hole in the basement wall."

Janie nodded sympathetically. "Yes, of course."

At the thought of the hole, I ignored a flutter of unease. I'd been back down in the basement a dozen times since Matt had given us the okay, mostly to move boxes from the cafe. Each time, the hole had gaped at me like an open wound. Getting it closed felt like the right thing to do. "I'll get mortar mix and other supplies this afternoon from the hardware store and ask Jerry for his help."

"Good idea." Janie pointed to the big chalkboard resting on the wall, which we'd soon be hanging up to display the menu. "While you're doing that, I can start writing our menu on the board."

I smiled. "*Your* menu, you mean."

She blushed. "At *your* cafe."

"At *our* cafe," I said immediately. "None of this could have happened without you."

"You know," she said, her voice brimming with affection, "I've really enjoyed this, Sarah. You and me, just like old times. It's been fun."

"I've had fun, too," I replied, surprising myself. Despite the aches and pains and my daily vociferous denunciations of a certain determined mayor, I realized I was glad I'd been maneuvered into doing this.

I pulled out my phone, fingers poised. "Last chance to change our minds before I tell everyone about tomorrow's soft opening."

Janie smiled. "Text away."

At that moment, the cafe door opened and Hialeah Truegood stuck her head in.

"Good morning," she said in her lovely Southern accent. "Do you have a few moments?"

"Of course, Hialeah. How can I help you?"

She stepped inside. Her silk dress today was a

rich azure long-sleeve number that complemented her tumble of red hair. "I saw this morning's paper and came right over."

"This morning's paper?" I asked, tensing.

Hialeah handed me a copy of the *Gazette*, her gaze anxious. "On the second page."

I sighed. The second page was where Bob ran his crazy editorials. "The *Gazette* is a local institution," I explained to her. "The owner is known to be a bit, um, eccentric at times."

I opened the paper to the second page and read:

In a free state, it is the duty of the press to speak truth to power. Doing so can be difficult when power avoids truth and hides behind lies.

The recent discovery of a body in a downtown building would appear, at first blush, to be the unfortunate consequence of a marriage gone bad. According to the tale being spun, a violent individual met a violent end. Upon hearing this account, many will conclude that justice was served.

But I am here to warn my fellow citizens: Do not fall for this convenient narrative!

There's much more to this situation — much we haven't been told. We are being deliberately misled by shadowy forces we know nothing about.

As always, citizens of Eagle Cove, I promise the Gazette will not rest until we uncover the full and complete truth.

I handed the paper to Janie, who read the editorial quickly and said, "Oh, dear."

"I think I can explain," I said to Hialeah. "The *Gazette* runs stuff like this all the time. The owner sees conspiracies everywhere. Most folks treat his editorials as a form of entertainment."

Our Southern visitor shook her head anxiously. "Sarah, that's not why I'm concerned."

"What do you mean?"

"I believe the *Gazette* is right."

"Right about what?"

"Shadowy forces *are* at work here," she said solemnly. "From the spirit world."

Oh, for crying out loud. I tried to keep my expression neutral. "The spirit world?"

"This building has known death and violence," she said, taking hold of my hands and squeezing tight. The day before, her touch had been light and feathery. But now I felt her strength, even her panic.

"Hialeah," I began.

"This building must be cleansed. I can do that. For your sake, for the sake of everyone here, I *must* do that."

"Cleansed?"

Her grip tightened. "It's why I was called here. At first I didn't understand, but now I do. Please, you must let me help you."

Again, I felt myself on the verge of saying no. This spirit talk was crazy nonsense — right?

"Hialeah," I said, carefully extricating myself from her grasp.

"I promise to stay out of your way," she said solemnly. "I will center my work at that table, near the front window. It's a spot of great energy. From there, I will commune with the spirits. I will beseech them to tell me where I need to focus my efforts."

I couldn't help it — I felt my curiosity stir. "What do those efforts involve?"

"Sage and special chants to banish the dark spirits."

"How long will it take?"

She shook her head. "There is no simple answer. The energy here is restless, unsettled. I sense anger, regret, sadness. But also a yearning for resolution."

I'll admit it — a shiver went through me as I absorbed her words. She seemed so *sincere*.

I glanced at Janie, who gave me a puzzled look that very clearly said, *This one is totally your call.*

"Listen," I said, collecting my thoughts. "I want to be honest with you. I don't know if I believe in what you're talking about."

"You're a non-believer," she said simply. "Most people are. I know that and accept that."

"That said, I've been on this planet long enough to understand that I don't know everything about everything. I've learned the hard way how important it is to stay humble and open."

Hope emerged in Hialeah's face. "Does that mean…?"

"I'm good with you trying to banish the bad spirits."

"Oh, I'm so glad," she said fervently. "I know this is a busy time for you." She cast her gaze over the cafe. "You've done so much in such a short time. You must be so proud."

"It's been a ton of work, but Janie and I are glad we did it."

"Would it be possible for me to begin later today?"

"Sure," I said. "We'll be in and out all afternoon — lots of last-minute stuff to do before we open tomorrow."

"Tomorrow?" she said, eyebrows rising. "Doesn't the festival begin in…?"

"In two days, that's right. Tomorrow is a soft opening. A test run."

"Such a smart idea. I promise to do my best to stay out of your way."

I checked my watch. "I should get going."

Hialeah took the hint and, after thanking us again, slipped away.

As soon as she was gone, I turned to Janie. "I don't know if I did the right thing."

Janie shrugged. "Who's to say?"

"We can always tell her to lay off if the chanting becomes too loud or weird."

Janie smiled. "I better get to the menu."

"And I better get to the hardware store."

As I prepared to head out, I remembered I'd left my handbag in my aunt's apartment and quickly dashed upstairs, feeling surprisingly full of energy. After letting myself in, I retrieved my handbag from the kitchen counter and found myself pausing to enjoy the sunlight streaming through the living room windows. My aunt's place seemed so airy and light during the day — so open and welcoming.

Then I heard it: a gentle *tap-tap-tap*. I went still, trying to identify the source. It didn't sound like a knock on the door — it was too soft for that. Perhaps it was Mr. Snuggles, climbing up the dumbwaiter shaft? Or maybe — ha ha — one of Hialeah's spirit pals? I pressed my ear to the closed dumbwaiter door and listened carefully but heard nothing.

Then I heard the tapping again. Was it coming from the hallway? I made my way to the entry foyer and was reaching for the door when something — instinct? premonition? — made me pause.

Instead of opening the apartment door, I peeked through the keyhole —

And saw Claire in the hallway, running a handheld device — like a phone with an antenna of some sort — over the wall.

I inhaled sharply. *What in the world?*

Not daring to move, I watched her slowly and

methodically scan every inch of the hallway's floor and walls.

Whatever it was she was after, she didn't find it. With a sigh, she flipped a switch on the device, folded it up, and slipped it into her handbag. After pausing to listen for movement or activity, she headed down the stairs to the second floor. A few seconds later, I heard the studio apartment door open and close.

I exhaled silently, forcing the tension out.

What was going on here?

What was Claire up to?

Things weren't adding up. *She* wasn't adding up.

And not just here and now.

My former best friend hadn't added up in *years*.

Heart thumping, I grabbed my handbag and slipped out of the apartment. As quietly as I could, I headed downstairs and got in my car.

I sat there silently, not ready to drive, trying to clear my head. I had a lot of thinking to do. A lot of *percolating* to do.

The body in the basement wasn't the only unknown here.

Another puzzle had appeared: The mystery of Claire.

And I wasn't going to stop until I figured her out.

CHAPTER 21

Which, of course, was easier said than done. Fifteen minutes later, I was still sitting in my car, motionless and anxious, unsure how to proceed. For reasons I wasn't clear about, my brain had decided it needed to review every single interaction I'd had with Claire over the past twenty years, collecting evidence to support a case I wasn't ready to admit I was building.

Out of the corner of my eye, I caught movement and sat up with a jolt. Claire had emerged from the building and was heading to her car, parked a few spots up from mine.

She hadn't seen me. Upstairs in the hallway, she'd been dressed in sweats, t-shirt, and slippers. Now she was wearing blue jeans, knee-high black boots, a cream wool sweater, and a black leather jacket — all effortlessly chic — and carrying what appeared to be a rifle bag over her shoulder. Her sports car's engine roared to life and she zoomed off.

With a gulp, my heart beating faster, I pulled out after her.

What was I doing? Was I *insane?* I'd never followed anyone. What if she saw me?

She was way ahead of me now — her car had tons of *oomph* — so I stepped on the gas and cast my memory back over decades of TV shows and movies, trying to recall the techniques I should use to avoid being noticed. The key, if I remembered right, was to stay far enough behind my target that she didn't notice me, but not so far behind that I lost her. Keeping a car or two between us was ideal — though at that moment, with the road mostly clear, that wasn't really possible.

Fortunately, as Claire turned off the main county road onto Old Winstead Lane, I realized where she was heading. I slowed, allowing her to zoom off, and followed at a sedate pace. The road was a two-lane affair through gently rolling hills, the afternoon sun adding a glow to the rows of apple trees in the surrounding orchard farms. I lowered the car window on impulse and was rewarded with the scent of fresh cider. With harvest season at its peak, every orchard in the region was working day and night to get their apples plucked and stored and processed before winter swept in.

A few minutes later, at the top of a hill overlooking Claire's parents' farmhouse, I pulled to the side of the road and hopped out to see what I could see. The farmhouse, white and plain in appearance but with a generous front porch, sat off the road at the end of a curved gravel drive about a quarter mile away. From this distance, Claire's red sports car parked out front was impossible to miss, as was the dark SUV next to it. Claire was standing next to the SUV, talking to the driver, a man in a dark suit. They were talking — no, scratch that. They were *arguing*. From the way Claire held her shoulders, I could tell she was irritated, even angry.

The man seemed upset, too. When the exchange ended abruptly, the man raised his window and roared away in a cloud of dust. As the SUV turned onto Old Winstead, I ran back to my car and hopped in, sinking low in my seat as he rushed by.

Why had I hidden from him? Was it because I was ashamed of my snooping? Or was something else at play, something I wasn't consciously aware of yet?

The question bounced through me as I started the engine and drove to the farmhouse. I'd followed Claire to find out what she was really up to, and I wasn't about to back away now.

The gravel drive crunched under my wheels. I

parked next to the sports car. Claire was nowhere to be seen. Had she gone inside?

Then I heard a shot and knew.

I walked around the farmhouse and found my former best friend out back, aiming her rifle at a row of cans she'd set on the posts of a fence a good football field away. She shifted the rifle slightly, zeroed in on her target, then —

Pop!

A can flew off the fence with a satisfying *ding*.

"Hey, Sarah," she said without turning around.

"Hey," I replied.

She readied her rifle for another shot. "What brings you out here?"

"I saw you leaving and decided to follow."

She aimed the rifle again, pressed the trigger — *pop!* — and another can went flying. She and her dad had done some hunting back in the day, but it was clear she'd upped her game.

"Nice shot," I said.

She swiveled toward me and held out the rifle. "Want to give it a go?"

I blinked, taken aback. I'd never fired a gun and had never really wanted to. Still….

"Sure," I heard myself say.

She handed me the rifle. It was heavier and more solid than I expected. I caught a whiff of what I guessed was gunpowder.

"I've never done this," I said.

"Try holding it the way I did."

I brought the rifle butt up to my shoulder and shifted my left hand under the barrel to support it.

She stepped forward and adjusted the end of the rifle so that it nestled in the crook of my shoulder. "Now try staring down the sight toward the target."

I leaned in and focused. Seeing the world from this viewpoint was a new experience for me. In an odd way, it felt empowering. Carefully, I aimed the rifle at one of the cans in the distance.

"Where'd you get the cans?" I asked her.

"Recycling bin. Now, tell me what you're seeing."

"I'm seeing the can in the center of the viewing thingie," I said, unsure of the words.

"Good," she said. "Slide your finger to the trigger, but don't pull it yet."

I inched my finger forward until I felt the trigger. "Okay, what now?"

"There'll be a kick," she said. "It might hurt."

"Hurt? How much?"

"Depends."

"I'm already sore and aching all over, thanks to the cafe prep."

She gave me a once-over to check my stance. "You're ready, I think. The way I approach this is, hitting a target is about finding your zone."

"Meaning?"

"It's about slipping into a state of consciousness or awareness where you're not thinking but instead knowing or sensing."

I frowned for a second, trying to process. "Like dancing?"

"Yes," she said, brightening. "It can be a lot like that. It's like your body or spirit knows."

"Okay." I took a deep breath, stretched my neck, and tried to settle in. A second passed, then another. I frowned. What she was suggesting was easier said than done. Where was my zone when I needed it?

"You're tense," she said. "What's going on?"

"I don't know," I said, getting irritated.

"Think Zen. You've got this."

I took another deep breath, then exhaled. "Who were you talking with?"

If the question surprised her, she didn't show it. "A colleague."

"It seemed like you were arguing."

"We were. He's a jerk."

"What were you arguing about?"

"The project I'm working on. There are issues."

"Why did he come all the way out here? Why not just call, or wait for you at Middlemore?"

She sighed. "I think he enjoys looking at me when he's yelling at me."

I called him a choice word and Claire chuckled. "Exactly."

In the rifle's line of sight, I was finding it easier to focus on the aluminum can. It was just a simple soda can, bought at a store, its contents consumed, destined to be recycled, until Claire plucked it from the garbage, took it to an empty field and placed it on a fence, where it was now waiting in the morning sun to be —

I pressed the trigger.

Bang! The rifle kicked my shoulder and —

The can went flying!

I cried out, stunned.

I'd actually hit the can?

"Wow," Claire said, impressed. "You nailed it!"

Adrenaline rushed through me along with pain. "I can't believe I did that."

"Are you holding back on me?" she said with a grin. "No one ever hits the target the first time out. Are you secretly an ace shot?"

I laughed and realized how much I'd missed this flow of connection between me and my childhood best friend. I'd loved how we were always in sync, attuned to the same wavelength, ready to face whatever the universe might throw at us —

"Why did you ditch me?" I blurted out.

Her cheeks flushed. "Sarah," she began.

"What happened?" I said, unable to stop myself. "It's like you decided one day to cut me off. And not just me. All of us."

She swallowed. "I know. I'm sorry. You're right."

When she didn't say more, I said, "Why did you do it?"

She swallowed again, staring at me.

I allowed the silence to lengthen, the rifle heavy in my hands. A minute earlier, shooting the gun had filled me with a sense of power and possibility. But now it felt like dead weight.

Claire blinked back tears. "I didn't plan it. I wasn't even really conscious of it at first. I was caught up in my new job. For a long while, work was my everything."

I kept my mouth shut, trying to use the silence to pry out more. I was going to need more than the "workaholic" excuse — a lot more.

"And then came the day I realized I hadn't talked with you in over a year."

She swallowed again. When I saw the guilt in her eyes, I felt a rush of emotion.

"It was the day Anna's birth announcement arrived in the mail. I realized I hadn't spoken with you even once during your pregnancy."

I blinked back tears, the old hurt resurfacing with a vengeance. Her abandonment of me during that deeply meaningful time had been inexplicable.

"I never understood that," I said, trying to keep my voice level.

"After a while, it became easier to *not* reach

out." She locked onto me as she said it, which was very Claire of her: Once she found her footing and picked a course of action, she didn't shy away.

"You had your life in California," she continued, "and I had mine in D.C. It became easier and easier to rationalize us falling out of each other's lives."

It hit me then, like a thunderbolt. *I knew why she'd done it.* My heart started racing. I nearly gasped aloud.

The truth that Claire had been keeping from me, the truth I'd been unwilling to accept until now, the truth that explained so much of what had been inexplicable for so long — was I right?

Yes. I felt it in my bones.

I blinked back tears, suddenly desperate to remain calm.

Claire was still talking — important words, judging by her expression — and I forced myself to focus on her. "I don't know how much this means to you now," she was saying, "but I'm sorry. I'm sorry I allowed this to happen. I'm sorry I didn't make the effort to reconnect. So many times over the years, I've wanted nothing more than to pick up the phone and talk with my best and oldest friend."

It was getting harder to hold back my tears. Was now the right moment to reveal that I knew? That I'd figured it out? That, weirdly enough, I no longer felt as angry?

No, my inner voice told me. Not now. Not yet. Her pain and regret were real. After all these years, she was opening up. If I confronted her now, she might feel compelled to hide the truth. And I didn't want that.

I didn't want to risk her pulling away. Not again.

"Thank you," I said. "I appreciate you saying that. It means a lot to me."

"I'm glad," she said, wiping away tears.

I stepped closer and handed her the rifle. "There's a lot more I'd like to talk about, but can I ask a favor?"

"Of course."

"Can we hit the pause button? I need a breather to absorb all of this. Plus, I have a ton of stuff to do before opening tomorrow."

"Of course," she said softly. "Congratulations on the cafe, by the way. You and Janie have been amazing."

"I should let you get back to your can attacks."

She gave me a small smile. "See you in town?"

"Count on it."

As I walked back to my car, I felt her watching my every step.

CHAPTER 22

Eagle Cove is a small town, but it definitely knows how to host a big show. Over the course of the next two days, under the careful direction of the Autumn Festival organizing committee, Main Street got gussied up in an exuberant and welcoming display of gold, red, and brown banners. The night before the festival began, the street was shut down to traffic and an army of volunteers descended to erect a stage for music and speeches, along with rows of tents for farmers, artists, and others to display their wares. Food carts were rolled into place, ready to offer hot dogs, pretzels, soft drinks, and more.

For Janie and me, the decision to open a day early proved a wise move. Almost immediately, we identified gaps in our planning — more singles needed for the cash register, more chocolate chip cookies required for the hungry hordes, along with dozens of other little tweaks — that kept us hopping. But we were also gratified to see how much we'd gotten right. All day and into the evening, a steady flow of folks stopped by to check out the cafe and thank us for supporting Eagle Cove.

I'll be honest: As tired and sore as I was, I felt good about what we'd accomplished. My resentment at being outmaneuvered by the mayor had faded, replaced by a sense of satisfaction at doing something good for my hometown.

Besides, keeping busy meant less time worrying about the body I'd found in the basement. Though I now believed I knew the broad strokes of what had happened, I still didn't know everything. For the moment, at least, additional digging would need to be put on hold.

At the crack of dawn on the day of the festival, I pulled myself from bed and hustled to the cafe, eager to get everything ready for our official debut. As soon as I placed the "Open" sign in the cafe's front door, customers started pouring in.

Gabby and her pals — Mrs. Bunch, Mrs. Chan, and Ms. Hollingsworth — were among the first to arrive. After perusing and discussing Janie's menu at length, they settled on hot tea and an assortment of scones and commandeered the booth closest to the front door. "You and Janie, you did good,"

Gabby said, surveying the space with approval. "Me and the girls, we'll be playing bridge, so don't bug us."

A short while later, Hialeah Truegood showed up in a gorgeous golden silk gown and set her things at a small table near the window. "A busy day for all of us," she said. "So many people have asked for readings."

The day before, I'd seen her waving sage in the building hallway, head bent in concentration.

"How goes the cleansing?" I asked.

"The spirits are aware of my presence," she said solemnly. "But they are not yet prepared to speak. When they are, I will be ready."

I heard a tap on the cafe window and found Jerry outside pushing a cart loaded with brick-laying supplies for the basement. I made my way through the cafe's side door into the building hallway, opened the front door to let him in, then helped him carry bricks and bags of sand and cement down to the basement.

As I set down a bag of cement mix, I couldn't help but shudder at the sight of the still-gaping hole in the basement wall.

"Don't be worried about that, Sarah," Jerry said. "The hole will be gone in no time."

I sighed. Was I that obvious? "Thank you, Jerry. You sure you don't want to do this after the festival?"

"If it's okay with you, I want to start filling in the hole this afternoon."

"Anytime you want. Whenever you're ready."

We were about to head up when I heard a familiar creak on the stairs and looked up to find Wendy Danvers on the top step.

"Wendy," I said, surprised. "What are you doing here?"

"Sarah," she said, taken aback. "I'm sorry, I didn't know you were here."

I resisted the impulse to accuse her of snooping. "And you're here because…?"

She hesitated, then squared her shoulders and continued down the stairs. "Okay, here's the deal. I was curious."

"Curious about what?"

"Everything." She cast her gaze around the basement as if trying to memorize every detail. "And not just because of my job at the *Gazette*."

"Then what for?"

Her voice rose with excitement. "I want to write a true-crime book. Narrative non-fiction. Something juicy."

Oh, geez. With difficulty, I kept my expression neutral.

"I mean, wouldn't that be incredible?" she continued. "Delving into what truly happened here, in this very basement, ten years ago?"

She was as curiosity-minded as I was, I realized.

But our motives couldn't be more different. She wanted a story, and I wanted — call me naive — the truth.

"Wendy," I said.

"Yes?"

"I'm not sure I want to dig up the past."

Liar, my inner truth-teller whispered.

"Really?" she said with a frown. "Don't you want to know what really happened down here?"

"I'm not sure I want everything to be made public."

"Things do get out eventually," she said, her gaze cool and frank. "I mean, just in terms of the reporting I've gathered for the *Gazette*, there's a lot about your great-aunt and this building that we haven't published yet."

Her threat was about as subtle as a tank. As levelly as I could, I said, "How about this? After the festival, let's sit down and talk."

"Does this mean I have your cooperation?"

"It means we can sit down and talk about what cooperation might entail." I gestured toward the stairs. "But this weekend is gonna be crazy-busy, so…."

Reluctantly, she took the hint. I followed her up to the hallway, Jerry a step behind, then ushered her into the cafe. "Janie's made some amazing treats. Please stop by anytime."

Wendy eyed me speculatively. "See you soon,

Sarah."

"Looking forward to it," I lied.

I heard my name and turned to see Mom and Mayor Johnson bustling toward me.

"Sarah," Mom said, pulling me in for a big, tight hug. "You did it! I'm so proud of you and Janie."

"Thank you," I said, resisting the inevitable urge to extricate myself from her over-enthusiastic embrace.

Mayor Johnson was beaming. "The two of you have done a wonderful job. Emily would be so proud."

"Thank you."

"No, Eagle Cove thanks *you*."

I gestured to Jerry, who was standing next to me. "Janie and I couldn't have done it without a lot of help, especially Jerry here."

Jerry gave us a self-conscious smile. "Happy to help."

"Jerry," Mayor Johnson said. "On behalf of Eagle Cove, I'd like to thank you as well." Then she glanced past Jerry's shoulder and frowned. "Who's that?"

I followed her gaze to the small table near the window, where Hialeah was pouring tea from a pot. "That's Hialeah Truegood," I said quietly. "She's from New Orleans. She does psychic readings."

"Hialeah?" Jerry repeated, puzzled.

The mayor blinked. "Readings? Here?"

"I figured she might bring in more foot traffic."

The mayor's expression cleared. "Excellent point, Sarah."

Hialeah must have heard us, because she beckoned for us to join her.

Just then, Janie called my name from the kitchen.

"Sorry," I said, "I'm needed in the back. You three, go introduce yourselves."

"Sarah," Mom said, "I have a bunch of stuff to do this morning, but I'll be back this afternoon to help out."

"Thanks, Mom."

And then, just like that, the morning became a rush of customers and a whirlwind of nonstop activity. Hordes of tourists descended onto Main Street to enjoy the beautiful autumn weather. Most of them, it seemed, needed coffee and scones to start their day. Before I could blink, the place was packed and Janie and I were inundated.

Indisputably, the cafe was a success. Amidst the crush, little moments stood out. From her favorite booth, Gabby announced that she and her friends were pleased. "We had our doubts, Sarah, but you and Janie pulled out a win!" Mr. Benson confided a particular fondness for Janie's maple-bacon scone. Matt stopped by to congratulate me, his expression proud and appreciative, before getting called away to help settle a parking dispute. Throughout the day, Hialeah did readings for a bunch of people, including Gabby, Mr. Benson, and Jerry. Wendy Danvers made an appearance, scribbling notes into her notebook. As promised, Mom returned around noon and assumed command of the front counter.

As the afternoon waned, the energy and flow finally slowed. The cafe was still busy, but the line for orders had melted away. For the thousandth time that day, I heard the bell of the cafe door. Claire strode toward me, a smile on her face.

"Congratulations!" she said. "How are you and Janie holding up?"

"I'm sure I'll be completely wiped out later, but right now I'm doing fine thanks to caffeine and adrenaline."

She gave me a smile. "I have some emails to take care of upstairs, but I'll come back down in a bit."

"Sounds good."

I watched her head through the cafe side door into the hallway. Since I'd confronted her at the farm, she'd been elusive — gone for long stretches, popping in and out at odd hours, always in a hurry.

But right now, at this very moment, I knew exactly where she was.

And, just as importantly, I'd figured out what I wanted to say to her and how I wanted to say it.

I ran my gaze over the space that Janie and I

had brought back to life, at the tables filled with happy tourists and gossiping locals, and breathed in the lovely aromas of coffee and baked goods. Janie bustled in from the kitchen with a fresh plate of cookies. At the register, Mom was happily chatting with a tourist and acting, at least for the moment, like her usual lively self. Outside, the crowds were starting to thin as the festival wound down for the day.

I pulled Janie aside. "Okay if I take a short break? I won't be gone long."

"Oh, sure, no worries," she said. "Things are slowing down. Everything's in hand."

"Thanks. Back soon."

I slipped into the hallway and made my way upstairs to the second floor, propelled by nervous anticipation.

Was I ready for this? Was I doing the right thing?

Only one way to find out.

Steeling myself, I knocked on the door to the studio apartment.

Claire opened the door. "Hey," she said.

For a split second, I paused. Did I really want to go through with this?

Yes, my inner voice said.

I straightened my posture and, keeping my gaze firmly fixed on her, said, very brightly:

"Hi, spy!"

CHAPTER 23

Claire's eyes widened a fraction, but otherwise her face remained immobile. For a long moment, she stared at me, not saying a word.

I gave her my biggest smile. "That's right, old pal. I figured it out!"

Her mouth tightened, which told me she was playing out the conversation that would inevitably follow, the one in which she professed ignorance or amusement or disdain or whatever tactic she deemed most likely to dissuade me from my conclusions, followed by me telling her to cut the bull.

Because that's the thing about being former best friends: She knew me well enough to know her lies wouldn't fly.

"We can talk about it out here in the hallway," I said, very loudly. "Or...."

She sighed. "You are impossible." She swung open the door. "Get in here."

With a flutter of excitement, I stepped inside, noting Claire's open suitcase on the dresser and her laptop on the small dining table. The studio apartment was tiny — not much bigger than a standard hotel room — but it was comfortably furnished and a pleasant refuge for occasional guests.

Claire grabbed her handbag from the bed and pulled out the same device I'd seen her use in the hallway two days earlier.

Without saying a word, she flipped open the device — close up, it looked pretty much like a mobile phone with a big antenna attached — and switched it on. I heard a faint hum.

She began running the device over me, starting at my head and moving down.

"You're checking me for a wire?" I said, amazed.

"Sorry," she said. "Force of habit."

I swallowed. "You think I…?"

She moved lower. "You've been meeting and greeting people all day. Plus, anyone can walk into the cafe. It's the easiest thing in the world to slip a bug in a pocket, or under a collar, or…."

I swallowed, simultaneously frightened and intrigued. "Quite a world you live in."

She bent down and moved the device over my legs.

A thought hit me — an idea so outlandish, it immediately became a certainty.

"Where'd you put *your* bugs?" I said.

The device paused over my sneakers, just for a second. Then she stood up, turned off the device, and directed her gaze at me. "Everywhere I thought I should."

I burst out with a laugh, unable to stop myself. "You're shameless."

"Just careful."

"I suppose that's a good thing in your line of work?"

She shrugged, clearly seeing no need to apologize.

I gestured to the dining table and chairs. "May I?"

"Please."

A bit shakily, I sat down. It wasn't every day you learn your oldest, dearest, closest childhood friend is

—

"CIA?" I asked.

After a brief pause, she said, "Yes."

I shook my head. "Try again. I know the CIA doesn't operate domestically."

Claire almost smiled. "Oh, you know that, do you?"

I paused, realizing I knew *nothing* about the strange world she apparently inhabited.

"Okay, how about this?" I said. "I'll pretend I believe you're with the CIA, at least for now. And you can pretend you've convinced me."

A genuine smile this time. "Deal."

I decided to start by confirming what I'd already guessed.

"You joined after college?"

She sat down opposite me. "Yes."

"And your consultant job is…."

"Cover."

"I have to say, you're taking all this — me barging in, I mean — rather well."

"I'm not happy about it," she said. "It complicates things. But I'm not surprised."

She appeared so poised sitting across the table from me. So calm and unruffled. She'd already decided what she was going to tell me, I realized.

Time to find out what that was. I took a deep breath. "Matt told us the victim's name was Peter Messina."

"That wasn't his real name," Claire said.

"Your agency put false information into the law-enforcement database?"

"Yes."

"Who was he? A criminal? A terrorist?"

She shook her head. "He was a colleague. I

worked with him and the woman he was here with."

"You mean Amy Messina?"

"They weren't married. That was their cover."

"What brought them to Eagle Cove?"

"Before I say more, please understand there's a lot I can't tell you. If my answers are vague, there are reasons."

"I understand."

"Okay," she said, sitting up in her chair. "Peter and Amy were assigned to uncover the source of a national security leak."

That was indeed *very* vague. "Go on."

"While investigating, they got into some sort of trouble."

"What sort of trouble?"

"We're not sure. We believe they were discovered and forced to hide out."

"Here in Eagle Cove?"

"That's right."

"Why here?"

"It's a quiet town, out of the way, but with a regular influx of tourists."

I tried to consider the town from the perspective of a spy on the run. "A place that's off the beaten path but accustomed to fresh new faces."

"We believe they came here to hide out…."

"Or they were following someone who was hiding out?"

"Yes."

"And then?"

"Apparently, they — or at least Amy — moved into this studio. And then they vanished. No communication, no evidence, no anything. Until you broke through that brick wall."

I swallowed. Clearly, I'd uncovered a lot more than a dried-out corpse when I picked up that sledgehammer.

She continued. "As soon as we heard about the body, we knew we had to investigate."

"And who better to send than you, the hometown girl?"

She shrugged, her gaze steady.

"Did you know them? Peter and Amy or whatever their real names were?"

I caught a flash of emotion. "I knew Peter — we trained together. Amy, no."

"Had you assumed they were dead?"

"That's always been the most likely explanation. For the past decade, there's been nothing about them. And by nothing, I mean *nothing*. It's like they vanished into thin air."

"Now that Peter's been found, what does that mean about Amy?"

"Most likely, it means she's dead."

"I'm sorry," I said.

"Sorry?"

"For your loss."

I watched her blink back tears that hadn't been there a second earlier. Behind her careful mask, I was catching a glimpse of the expressive friend I'd once had.

"Thank you," she said. "I appreciate you saying that."

"You and Peter — you had a relationship, didn't you?"

"For about a year after college, during our training. It didn't last, but...."

"But you still had feelings for him."

"There are some guys you never really get over." Her gaze intensified. "Isn't that right?"

She wasn't talking about herself anymore. Hurriedly, before she could send me tumbling down that particular rabbit hole, I said, "I know you can't reveal anything about the leak. But did the information eventually get used or revealed?"

She paused, weighing her answer. "Some of it, yes."

"But some of it, no?"

"That's right."

"So maybe whoever killed Peter and presumably Amy got their hands on some of the information but not all of it?"

She stayed silent, waiting for me to continue.

"So now," I said, "one of the reasons you're here is to see if Peter and Amy got their hands on the information and left it here, hidden away in this building?"

"That's right."

"Your scanner thingie," I said, pointing to the device. "I'm guessing it's strong enough to see through walls?"

She sighed. "You saw me."

"Two days ago. Through the keyhole."

"Let's just say it does what you think it does."

"So it's some kind of secret tech?"

"Yes."

"Keeping it vague? Okay, fine." A thought came. "Do you think whoever killed Peter might come back for the information now that Peter's body's been discovered?"

"We don't know. Possibly, yes. Most likely, no. Whoever did this got away with murder. The smart decision would be to stay away."

Her assessment sounded right. In fact, everything Claire was telling me sounded right. In her deliberately vague way, I sensed she was telling me the truth. Peter and Amy had been fellow agents on a case. Something had gone wrong and Peter (and presumably Amy) had been killed.

"Would the killer or killers be worried about something else being uncovered here in the building?" I asked. "Could that worry them enough to come back?"

"Perhaps," she said. "What Matt told you about being careful? It's very good advice."

Without a doubt she was right. And yet –

"Sarah," my former best friend said, interrupting my train of thought. "We've known each other forever. I know you'll want to go digging."

I resisted my instinctive urge to protest. Because what was the point? Even after all these years, my friends had my number. "Fine. I get it. National security. Killer on the loose. I'll back off. But there's one thing I don't get."

"What's that?"

"Why Aunt Emily wrote that letter." I was about to say more when I brought myself up short: I hadn't told Claire about the letter.

"That's a bit of a puzzle," Claire said.

I blinked in surprise. "You know about the letter?"

"Yes."

"But I didn't tell you."

She waited for me to catch up.

"You found out by *spying* on me?"

"Part of the job," she said, almost cheerfully.

I stared, speechless. Why was I so shocked? For two days, I'd known she worked as some sort of secret government agent. It made perfect sense that, as a spy, she would spend at least some of her time *spying*.

But on *me?* As her former best friend, didn't I warrant more respect?

"I want you to stop spying on me," I said.

She nodded. "Sure, no problem."

"It's that easy?"

"Yep, that easy."

"That's a lie, right?"

She smiled. "Of course not." Then her smile grew wider.

"Fine," I said, half-frustrated and half-amused by the way she was toying with me. "Go ahead, be inscrutable. I suppose I'll just have to deal?"

"That's usually the best approach. Okay if I switch topics?"

"Sure."

She shifted in her seat. "About Emily's letter…. You asked a good question. Do you have it with you? Can I see it?"

I pulled out my phone and showed her the photo I'd taken. Claire read it carefully.

"Emily's handwriting?"

"Yes."

"Jim Atkins confirmed that Emily was the one who gave him the letter?"

"That's right." A thought came. "You're not suggesting that Jim Atkins is involved?"

"Not at all," she replied immediately. "To the best of my knowledge, he's exactly what he appears to be — an honest, capable, small-town lawyer."

"What about the rest of us?"

"What do you mean?"

"Have you checked out the rest of us, too?"

"Oh," she said, getting it. "Yes, completely and totally. Everyone here."

"What about the newcomers? Like Wendy Danvers, the reporter at the *Gazette*?"

"Nothing unusual in her background. Just like everyone else."

Inspiration struck. "Even Hialeah Truegood?"

Claire smiled. "Yes, even her."

"Tell me you're joking. She's the real deal?"

"I can't speak to the accuracy of her psychic predictions, but she's been a professional medium in New Orleans for twenty years. Two decades of tax returns, a Web site for more than a decade, years of activity on social media…."

I shook my head. "Color me surprised."

"It's always important to check."

I frowned. "What did you find out about me?"

Her smile faded. She weighed her words before speaking. "Only that you've had a rough couple of years."

I wasn't sure how to respond. She was right, of course. "It's been rough," I finally said. "But I'm ready to move forward."

"Emily would have liked that answer."

"Which brings us back to her, and why she

wrote that letter." I took a deep breath. "Do you think she killed Peter?"

"No," Claire said. "Not a chance."

At the sound of those simple words, relief flooded through me and I found myself blinking back tears. Until that second, I hadn't truly appreciated how much I hated the idea of Emily killing Peter.

I cleared my throat. "But she did help cover up his death and hide his body. That part of her letter was true."

"Without a doubt," Claire said. "The question is why. I can see her writing the letter if she believed she was doing the right thing."

"Emily was always a firm believer in doing the right thing."

Claire's lips tightened. "Maybe the killer pressured her into writing the letter. Maybe she cooperated to protect you and your family."

"Or protect Amy," I said quietly.

"I've wondered the same." My friend went quiet and I got the strong sense there was more she wanted to say.

After making a mental note to circle back later, I said, "Maybe we're overthinking this. Maybe the letter is exactly what it seems: an attempt by Emily to protect her tenants and Amy from being investigated as suspects, should the body someday be discovered."

Claire sighed. "Sometimes the simplest answer is the best answer."

"So is that our working theory? Somebody killed Peter, and Emily chose to hide Peter's body, possibly to prevent harm to herself or others, and wrote the letter to let Gabby and Mr. Benson and Amy off the hook?"

"Could be."

"There's something you should know." Briefly, I told her what Gabby and Mr. Benson had told me about Amy leaving the day after Peter's death.

Claire listened closely. "It's likely she didn't get far."

I swallowed. "You mean, whoever killed Peter followed Amy and…?"

Claire's expression was grim. "We haven't heard a thing from her in ten years."

There were so many layers to this, I realized. "How do you keep track?"

Her brow furrowed. "Of what?"

"The lies. They keep coming nonstop. All the time."

She gave me a sad smile. "It isn't easy."

"Say Emily did what she did under coercion to protect others. She would have hated being pressured into silence. She would have wanted to get out from under that. Why didn't she go to the authorities?"

"A good question."

Another thought hit. "Maybe it's even simpler. What if Amy showed up as a domestic abuse victim and Emily bought her story? Maybe Amy said she killed Peter in self-defense, and Emily believed her?"

Once again, I could sense Claire holding back. "I doubt that's what happened."

I sighed. "If I come up with a better theory, I'll let you know."

"Sarah."

"What?"

"You know what I'm going to say."

"That I need to stay out of this."

"No hunting down facts to support theories about what might have happened ten years ago."

"I'm out of it. Promise. No hunting."

She seemed unconvinced. "For real?"

"Yes, for real."

"Thank you. And it goes without saying…."

"Keep it zipped."

"Right."

I stood up. "I should get back downstairs."

Claire rose and followed me to the door.

"Okay if I come back up later?" I asked her. "There's lots more I want to talk about."

"Text me first. I may need to go back to Middlemore."

"For real? You really have a project at Middlemore?"

She smiled. "Not the one I told you about, but yes, I'm working on something there."

"Which you can't tell me about."

"You learn fast." She opened the door and I slipped out.

I turned to face her. "Because of national security blah blah blah."

That amused her. "Yes, top-secret hush-hush blah blah blah."

We grinned at each other as she gently closed the door.

On my way down the stairs, I heard a sound I couldn't identify, coming from the direction of the basement.

Then I remembered: Jerry was down there, bricking up the hole in the wall.

Perhaps he'd like something from the cafe?

I went to the basement door and called down, "Hey, Jerry. Anything I can get you? Coffee? Muffin?"

I waited, expecting a response, but was met with silence.

"Jerry?" I said again.

I frowned. The light was on, but I couldn't see him from where I stood. If Jerry wasn't down there, then what had made the noise? Perhaps Mr. Snuggles had knocked something over while surveying his territory?

With mounting trepidation, I made my way down, each wooden step creaking under my weight.

"Jerry, you down here?" I asked again.

When I reached the foot of the stairs, I turned and saw —

My heart skipped a beat —

Jerry —

On the ground —

Motionless.

"Jerry!" I cried, moving forward.

Then I felt it —

A sharp pain in my neck.

Suddenly, I couldn't see straight.

I fell to the floor and tumbled into —

Darkness.

CHAPTER 24

Like a light switching on, consciousness flooded through me.

I was on the ground. In Matt's arms.

Why was I in Matt's arms?

"Sarah," I heard him whispering urgently, even fearfully. "Can you hear me?"

I struggled to focus. "What happened?"

"You're gonna be okay," he said as he gazed down at me, anxiety etched on his face, fear cracking his voice. "You're gonna be just fine."

I was in the basement. The floor beneath me felt cold, the cement rough to the touch. I tried sitting up but immediately fell back as the world went blurry. "Matt…."

"Don't move, Sarah. I want you to stay still."

Shakily, my hand rose to his face. Everything felt hazy and slow. My fingers traced the line of his jaw. His skin was warm, his stubble rough.

Why was everything moving in slow-motion?

Without warning, memories came rushing back —Jerry on the ground, the pain on my neck — and I gasped.

"Jerry!" I cried, trying to sit up again, my heart racing like a jackhammer. "He's been hurt."

"I know," Matt said.

A wave of dizziness hit me and I collapsed back into his arms. "I feel…."

"Like you've been drugged?"

"Drugged?" My hand went to my neck, my fingers finding what felt like a welt.

Tears spilled down my cheeks. I was remembering it now — all of it. I turned my head, dreading what I knew I would see.

A few feet away, Jerry Meachum lay on his back, unnaturally still. He might have been asleep except his chest wasn't moving. He was staring upward, seeing nothing.

"He's dead," I whispered.

"I'm sorry," Matt said.

"I found him." My voice was scratchy, hoarse. "I wanted to see how he was doing with the…." My gaze slid to the still-gaping hole in the wall.

"When you came down, what did you see?"

"I saw him on the floor."

"Anything else?"

I shook my head. "I was going to him when I felt a pain in my neck."

"What brought you down here?"

"I was in the hallway. I heard a noise. I decided to check on him. But he was already on the ground. That means the noise was made by…."

His voice rose with anger. "Someone shot you with a dart."

"A dart?"

"Judging by the puncture mark. Dosed with some kind of knockout drug. When I saw you on the ground, I…."

"Hey," I said, moving my hand to squeeze his arm. "I'm still here."

"We're going to get you checked out to make sure you're okay. Help is on the way."

An alarming thought hit. "What about everyone else?"

"They're fine," he said immediately. "Everyone's fine."

"Mom? Janie? The folks in the cafe?"

"All fine. A deputy is with them."

"What about Claire? I was upstairs with her."

His brow furrowed. "You didn't come here from the cafe?"

"I was with Claire in the studio apartment."

"How long were you up there?"

"Fifteen, twenty minutes?"

"Do you know what time Jerry came down here?"

I tried recalling. Jerry had popped into the cafe sometime that afternoon, but did I remember when?

"Sorry," I said. "He stopped by, but I didn't note the time. We were so busy."

"No worries."

"Why are you here?"

"I came to see you." He hesitated, which told me he'd decided that now was not the time to tell me whatever it was he'd come here to tell me. "You weren't in the cafe, and Janie told me you were taking a break. I was heading up to Emily's apartment when I noticed the basement door open and decided to see if you were here and...."

He was going to have a tough time investigating what had just happened, I realized. The hallway was easily accessible from the cafe. With the cafe packed and the Harvest Festival in full swing, slipping into the basement unnoticed would have been a snap.

"How did Jerry die?" I asked.

He shook his head slowly as he gazed at me, his concern now tinged with relief. "You must be starting to feel better."

"Matt, please tell me."

"He was shot with a dart, same as you. Then the killer bashed in the side of his head."

"With what?" I gasped.

"A brick."

More tears came. "I asked him to help me fill in the hole."

"I know."

"The hole I made."

"Sarah."

"This is my fault."

"No," he said vehemently. "This is the *killer's* fault."

"The killer wouldn't have come back if I hadn't knocked that hole in the wall."

He went still. "What do you mean?"

Uh oh. I recognized that tone. What had I just revealed?

"Hmm?" I said, trying to retreat into faux fuzziness.

"What do you mean, the killer wouldn't have come *back*?"

I was going to blame the dart, I decided. The drug in the dart was turning me into a blabbermouth.

"Did I say that?" I said vaguely.

"What was the killer coming back for?"

"Hmm?"

He shook his head, clearly not pleased. My feeble act wasn't cutting it. And the problem was, the urge to confide in him was overwhelming. I felt like a leaky sieve. Adding to my state of susceptibility was the undeniable fact that being held in his arms felt really, really *good*. He was so strong and solid. He made me feel so *safe*.

The clomp of footsteps on the basement stairs saved me from revealing more. Doc Barnes appeared and knelt at my side.

"Ms. Boone, we have to stop meeting like this."

"No argument from me," I replied.

Other footsteps followed — Deputy Wilkerson and someone else — as Doc Barnes checked my pulse and heart rate and aimed a light in my eyes.

"Are we ready upstairs?" Matt asked the deputy, who was setting down floodlights and crime-scene tape on the ground.

"The building and cafe are cordoned off, and we've told everyone in the cafe they have to stay here until we question them."

"There are three tenants on the second floor. If they're not already in the cafe, make sure they're available for questioning as well."

"Got it," Deputy Wilkerson said, and dashed off.

"Sarah," Matt said, "we're going to get you to the clinic now."

"I don't need to go there," I said, trying to sit up.

"No arguments," Doc Barnes said. "That's an order."

Despite my protests, they wouldn't let me try to

stand. I watched with annoyance and resignation as paramedics maneuvered a weird stretcher-chair down the basement steps. Then they lifted me into it — again, totally unnecessarily — and carried me upstairs like a captive invalid.

In the hallway, Deputy Martinez was holding back an anxious crowd at the cafe door.

"Sarah!" Mom cried as I was wheeled by. "Tell me you're okay."

"I'm fine, Mom."

"Are they taking you to the clinic?"

"Yes," one of the paramedics said.

Mom slipped under Deputy Martinez's arm. "I'm going with you."

Deputy Martinez reached for her. "Ma'am —"

"Don't you dare Ma'am me, young lady. My daughter's been attacked. She needs me!"

"You tell 'em, Nancy!" I heard Gabby yell from inside the cafe.

"It's okay, Deputy," I heard Matt say. "We'll get Nancy's statement later."

I glanced up behind me and saw Matt gazing at me with concern and affection.

"I feel like an idiot in this chair," I said.

"Tough," he said, softening the word with a smile. "I'll check in with you later."

CHAPTER 25

The next three hours were a typical slog through the medical system. At the clinic, a nurse drew my blood and x-rayed my head and aimed lights in my eyes and asked me a dozen times what day my birthday was.

Finally, when I managed to satisfy her that I hadn't cracked my skull in half, she allowed Mom to take me home. My first instinct was to go upstairs and crash, but Mom ordered me into the kitchen and sat me down at the table while she warmed up a pot of her homemade chicken noodle soup (utterly delicious, by the way) while talking nonstop about everything except what had just happened. After watching me down a hearty bowl, she handed me my phone and allowed me to reply to anxious texts from Janie, Claire, Gabby, and Mr. Benson.

Then she listened as I called Anna and Grace and told them what had happened.

With all of them, the conversations went something like this:

Yes, I was fine. I still felt hazy from the drug, but otherwise I was okay.

Yes, Mom was taking excellent care of me.

No, I had no idea who'd drugged me and killed Jerry.

No, I had no idea why anyone would want Jerry dead.

No, I had no intention of ever setting foot in that basement again.

Yes, I was going to get a good night's sleep.

No, I didn't need anything — all was in hand.

Yes, I'd call them first thing tomorrow to check in.

Finally, after the communications frenzy ended, I set down the phone. "I think I'll head up to bed."

"Not yet," Mom said. "The nurse told me to keep you awake for another four hours."

"Mom…."

"No arguing, Sarah."

"My head is fine. No concussion, no nothing."

"Apparently your ears aren't working right."

"Fine," I groused, feeling once again like a recalcitrant teenager, chafing under autocratic parental authority. "But Mom, we need to talk about Aunt Emily."

She stiffened. "Why?"

I took a deep breath and told her about Emily's letter. Mom listened in silence, then shook her head.

"It didn't happen that way."

"What do you mean?"

The question seemed to fluster her. "I mean, it couldn't have."

"Why do you say that?"

"Because I know her. She wouldn't have shot him."

I frowned. "Why not? Even to defend herself?"

"She would have found another way."

"Another way to…?"

"Stop him."

I stared at her, unsure how to respond. Mom seemed so *sure*. Her faith in Emily was understandable — my aunt had been nothing if not resourceful — but why was she so quick to reject the evidence presented by Emily herself and supported by Gabby and Mr. Benson?

"The wife probably did it," Mom added.

"I agree with you," I said evenly. "But I think it's inescapable that Emily helped cover up the man's death."

"Oh, that," Mom said, brushing the point away. "If that's what happened, then I'm sure she had her reasons."

A truly shocking thought hit me. *Could it be?*

I took a deep breath. "You knew."

Mom frowned. "Don't be silly."

"Aunt Emily told you what happened."

Mom shook her head, clearly unhappy with me. "I don't want to talk about this anymore."

"Mom, what else did she tell you?"

Mom's lips started trembling. "Sarah, I am trying to be strong. Strong like you, strong like Emily. But all of this — it's too much. Emily gone, you attacked, poor Jerry killed…."

I swallowed back a rush of tears. "Mom, I'm sorry. I shouldn't have pushed."

She reached out and took my hands in hers. "Right now, Sarah, I need to have my daughter here with me, *not* asking questions. The past is the past. I need you to *not* go digging."

"Of course," I said immediately. "I'm sorry for all of this."

"Don't be sorry. What happened is not your fault. You have nothing to apologize for."

I found myself returning to the memory of Jerry on the cold basement floor. "I wish I could believe that."

"You *need* to believe that. You didn't kill him."

I barely managed to avoid uttering the thought that came next: *But I'm going to find out who did.* The drug in my system was still playing havoc with my usual inhibitions and emotions. The nurse at the clinic had told me I'd feel residual effects for the next day.

I gave Mom's hands a squeeze. "How about we go into the living room and watch TV?"

"I'd like that," she said with a smile.

As we rose from the table, my phone buzzed.

"It's Matt," I said. "I should…."

Mom wasn't pleased. "Keep it short."

I picked up. "Hey."

"Hey, Sarah," he said, his voice low and rumbly and concerned. "How are you feeling?"

"Tired, to be honest. Drained."

"Everything check out at the clinic?"

"Everything's fine. No concussion. As a precaution, the nurse told Mom she needs to keep me awake for the next four hours. Mom fed me some of her famous chicken-noodle soup, and now we're going to watch some TV."

"Good. I'm glad." His voice thickened. "When I saw you on the ground, I…."

"Hey," I said, touched. "I'm fine. Promise."

"Good." He paused. "You got a minute to chat?"

I glanced at Mom. "Sure, a couple of minutes."

Mom frowned, then started clearing the table.

"First, anything else you remember about what happened?"

I didn't answer right away, trying to draw forth even a scrap of fresh detail. "I'm sorry," I finally said. "Beyond what I already told you, I got nothing."

"That's okay. No worries."

"Is there a reason you're asking? Is there a new lead?"

Again, I sensed him hesitating whether to tell me. "I have a question for you and Nancy. About Emily."

"Sure," I said. "Ask away."

"Emily was on the road to Middlemore when she had her crash. Any idea what she might have been doing over there, or who she might have been visiting?"

"Grace lives in Middlemore," I said. "Maybe she was going to see her and the kids. Want me to ask Mom?"

"Yes, please."

I repeated Matt's question and Mom shook her head. "Sorry, I don't know. But she wouldn't have been going to see Grace or the kids that day. They were here for a soccer tournament."

I repeated that to Matt, then said, "Why are you asking about Emily?"

This time, the pause went longer.

"Matt," I said. "Tell me."

He let out a sigh. "Sarah, I've dispatched a deputy to watch your house tonight."

Fear jolted through me. Mom was at the sink now, rinsing the dishes, the rush of water loud and strong. Quietly, I said, "Why?"

"It's only a precaution," he said.

"Matt, tell me why."

"The reason I had to cancel our coffee the other day is that I've been trying to get a crane up to the ridge road to pull up Emily's car."

I blinked, startled. "And?"

"Two days ago, we finally managed to borrow a crane from a construction site and retrieve the car and get it in for analysis."

I gulped. "And?"

"The car was smashed up and badly burned — no surprises there." I heard him take a deep breath. "But on one side of the car, we found car paint."

I frowned, not getting it. "What do you mean?"

"From another car."

A strange feeling washed over me. Trembling, I sat down, suddenly lightheaded, my body responding before my brain could process what he was saying.

"Another car?" I repeated.

"Sarah, I'm sorry."

"What are you saying?"

He took a deep breath. "What I'm saying is…."

As I waited for the words that I knew would come next, tears started flowing.

"Somebody ran Emily off the road deliberately."

CHAPTER 26

I kept Matt's revelation from Mom. At first, I didn't understand why.

After ending the call, as Mom and I settled onto the sofa in the living room, Mom asked me what I'd meant by "another car." I told her Matt was finishing up his report on Emily and hoping to find a car that may have been on the road at the same time.

Strictly speaking, that wasn't a lie. But it also wasn't the truth. In that moment, I told myself I was shielding her from the truth to protect her.

But the reality was — and I understood this only later, after much reflection — I was shielding *me* from *Mom*. Already, deep in my bones, I knew I wouldn't rest until I found Emily's killer. As soon as Mom figured that out, she'd do everything she could to dissuade me, including glomming onto me and never letting me out of her sight.

So after three hours of TV that I barely paid attention to, Mom finally allowed me to go to bed. As I lay my weary head down to sleep, I hoped my dreams would be vivid and insightful and point me to the solution.

Alas, I slept like a log — no dreams, no insights — and awoke to sunlight streaming through my bedroom window. I struggled out of bed, stepped to my usual spot in front of the wall mirror, and stared with dismay at the nasty bruise blossoming on my neck, courtesy of the dart.

After changing into jeans, sweatshirt, and house slippers, I went downstairs and found Mom in the kitchen.

"Morning," I said.

She slid me a cup of coffee. "How are you feeling?"

"Pretty good. I slept well."

The mug was toasty warm in my hands, the aroma of the coffee drawing me in.

Mom's gaze landed on my neck. "Oh, that must hurt." She stepped closer. "Does it?"

"It's tender to the touch, but otherwise...."

"We'll take it easy today. You need to stay quiet and rest up."

"I don't suppose Janie and I can open the cafe for the last day of the festival?"

She shook her head. "Sorry, Matthew shut you down."

I sighed, not surprised. "Anything from him this morning?"

"Not yet. But I talked to Betsy, and she said the blood results came back. You were shot with a drug used to tranquilize large animals."

"Large animals?"

"Like horses. The good news is, the effects dissipate quickly." She moved back to the stove. "Let me make you some eggs and bacon."

"Thank you."

I was about to sit down at the kitchen table when I heard a knock at the front door. "I'll get it."

"If it's Matthew, tell him I have breakfast for him."

I opened the door and was surprised to find Eddie the mailman.

"Good morning, Eddie," I said cautiously.

He handed me a stack of letters, along with a large manila envelope. "That one's special delivery."

"Who from?"

"Jim Atkins."

"You need to see my ID?"

"Once is enough," he said, then turned to leave. "Gotta go. Route to finish."

I realized something. "Eddie, can I ask you a question?"

"What?" he asked, pausing reluctantly on the sidewalk.

As quietly as I could, I pulled the front door shut behind me and stepped onto the porch. "When we met, I asked if you'd met Peter Messina."

"That's right, you asked that."

"You said you hadn't. But when I asked that, you remembered you'd met his wife Amy, didn't you?"

He nodded. "She got a package at the cafe."

"Is there a reason you remembered that?"

The question seemed to puzzle him. "I don't know." A frown appeared. "Maybe. Now you've got me thinking."

"Thinking?"

"Wondering." He shook his head. "Now it's going to bug me."

"What is?"

"Your question."

"I'm sorry. I didn't mean to bug you."

"Well," he said sourly, "you just did."

Without another word, he marched off.

I watched his mail truck rumble away, unsure what to make of that, then looked at the manila envelope in my hand.

Why would Jim Atkins send me a ...?

My heart thumped. A delivery from Jim Atkins might mean —

Another letter from Aunt Emily?

I tore open the manila envelope. Inside was a smaller envelope, with five words on it in my aunt's familiar handwriting: *Sarah — for your eyes only*.

With trembling fingers, I opened the envelope, extracted a single sheet of paper, and read:

> *Sarah,*
> *Look where I haven't been.*
> *Use if needed.*
> *It has no value, but they won't know that.*
> *With all my love, Emily*

I swallowed, this time with bewilderment. *Aunt Emily, what in the world is this about?*

I was shivering, I realized. The morning air was sharp. Winter was coming. From the ground below, cold seeped into my slippers.

The letter was a riddle, obviously. A puzzle I was meant to solve.

But how?

Frustration, even annoyance, crept in. How was I supposed to know where my aunt *hadn't* been?

What was I supposed to *use*?

What was *it*?

Who were *they*?

I shook my head, chastising myself. There was zero point in getting upset. Emily wasn't being cryptic to mess with me — that wasn't her style. She was being cryptic because she believed she *had* to be. Whatever she hoped to communicate, she hoped to communicate only to me.

A thought came: Why had this letter been delivered *now*?

I stood there in the cold air, chewing on my next steps. I wasn't going to tell Mom about this second letter, at least not until I knew what it meant. After taking a deep breath, I pulled my phone from my pocket and called Jim Atkins.

He picked up on the second ring. "Hello, Sarah."

"Jim," I said, "you know why I'm calling."

"I do."

"I assume Aunt Emily left instructions on when to send this second letter?"

"Correct."

"What were her instructions?"

"Her instructions were to send the letter only after the first letter was sent, in the event of a disturbance of any sort in your building. A break-in, burglary — anything warranting the involvement of the sheriff."

I flashed to the image of Jerry's lifeless body on the basement floor and pushed back a rush of anger.

"Jim, are there more letters?"

"That," he said carefully, "is something I'm not at liberty to disclose."

Which meant there were. "Can't you just hand them over to me?"

"Sarah, I can't even confirm their existence to you."

I nearly grunted in frustration. *What game was Aunt Emily playing?* What secrets required her to communicate with me — and only me — from the grave? How many more letters had she written?

"Jim," I said, "what was Emily involved with in Middlemore?"

"The town? The university?"

"I'm not sure. Either."

He paused to consider. "Nothing I'm aware of. Why do you ask?"

"She was on the road to Middlemore when she had her crash. I'm wondering why."

He was silent for a moment. "I'm afraid I can't help with that. Not because I'm constrained in any manner, but because I don't know." He cleared his throat. "Sarah, as your attorney, I need to ask: Is there anything in the second letter I should know about?"

"I don't think so," I said slowly. "You'll be relieved to hear she didn't confess to a second killing. In fact, she didn't mention any crime at all."

"I'm relieved to hear that. Are you all right? I heard what happened yesterday. A dreadful business."

"I'm fine."

"Let me know if there's anything I can do to help."

"Thanks, Jim. Will do."

I hung up. Aside from being in way over my head, caught in a dangerous world I knew nothing about, what did I know?

It was time to be methodical — to take a deep breath and get into my zone.

After folding up the manila envelope and stuffing it into my jeans pocket, I returned to the kitchen, handed Mom the rest of the mail, and sat down at the table to eat my breakfast.

"Who was at the door?" Mom asked.

"Eddie the mailman."

"He doesn't usually knock."

"Maybe he heard what happened and wanted to see for himself how I was doing," I said, the lie coming easily.

Mom nodded — curiosity as a motive made sense to her. "What do you feel like doing today?"

"I'm not sure. But would it be okay if I went upstairs and took a nap for a bit?"

"Are you feeling okay?"

"Fine," I said immediately. "Promise. Just a bit tired."

"How about this? While you're napping, I'll drop something off at the office and pop over to the store and get things for dinner. Then we can settle in for a nice quiet day."

"Sounds good." I stood up. "See you in a bit."

Upstairs, I initially did exactly what I told Mom I'd do: I lay down on the bed and tried to open my mind to any and all random thoughts. A short while later, when I heard Mom head out, I sat up and reached for my laptop.

It was time to put some organization to the jumble of facts bouncing around my head. I stared at the blank screen, fingers poised. If Claire was telling me the truth — and for the moment, I was choosing to believe her — then what I knew was:

1. A decade ago, information vital to national security had been stolen.
2. Peter and Amy, undercover government agents, showed up in Eagle Cove.
3. Emily let Amy stay in the studio apartment.
4. Emily and Peter had an intense discussion outside the cafe.
5. Somebody killed Peter.
6. Emily closed the cafe and, with help from Gabby and Mr. Benson, hid Peter's body in the basement.
7. Emily wrote a letter, addressed to me, in which she confessed to the killing, most likely to keep her friends out of trouble.
8. A decade later, somebody ran Emily off the road.

9. I unearthed Peter's body in the basement.

10. Claire showed up, asked to stay in the studio apartment, and began searching the building for anything related to the stolen information.

11. Somebody murdered Jerry and shot me with a dart gun. The dart marks on our necks appeared to match a mark on Peter Messina's body.

12. And now a second letter from Emily had arrived.

I paused and read what I'd just typed. What did all of this mean? What did it suggest?

One thing leaped out: Not only had Emily anticipated the possibility of Peter's body being discovered, she'd understood that the discovery might prompt dangerous people to target the building.

Which raised the question: Had Emily also known about the stolen information? Not necessarily, I realized. It was possible that Amy told her she was on the run from bad guys who wanted something she or Peter had stolen — money or jewels, perhaps.

Still, it was clear that Emily knew danger was afoot. Her second letter was a warning: *Bad guys were here.* It was also a map to something that might prove helpful.

Which led to another inescapable conclusion: Somehow, Emily expected *me* to figure it all out.

With a sigh, I picked up the letter and reread it yet again.

Aunt Emily, you expected too much.

Idly, my gaze wandered over the bedroom and landed on my open suitcase in the middle of the floor. Messy clothes spilled over the sides. At some point, I was going to have to sort through the pile of clothes and decide which items needed a good wash, then get everything folded and restored to a semblance of order.

Peeking from beneath a dirty sweatshirt, I spied the ribbon holding together the packet of Aunt Emily's postcards.

My brain stirred.

Look where I haven't been….

What if…?

I jumped up, retrieved the postcards from my suitcase, and sat back down on the bed. With trembling fingers, I loosened the ribbon holding the packet together and spread the colorful postcards out before me. Aunt Emily and Uncle Ted had visited so many places during their years abroad. In their unique way, these postcards represented a record of her travels.

And then — I restrained a gasp — I knew what Emily wanted me to do. With a surge of excitement, I gathered the postcards together and stood up. Mom would be back soon, but if I hurried, I might be able to get back before she returned.

In the downstairs hallway, I tossed off my slippers, slipped into sneakers, grabbed my handbag and keys, and dashed out the door.

CHAPTER 27

With the second day of the Harvest Festival in full swing, I was forced to park three blocks from the cafe. As quickly as I could, I slipped through the crowds, cringing as I caught my reflection in a storefront window. I was a *mess*. I looked exactly like I'd just rolled out of bed, thrown on jeans and a sweatshirt, and dashed out of the house without even a second's thought about my appearance.

Miraculously, I managed to avoid running into anyone I knew, though at one point I had to duck to avoid being spotted by Wendy Danvers, who doubtless would have wanted to ambush me for a quote for the *Gazette*.

When I finally reached my aunt's building, I unlocked the hallway entry door and pushed my way in, exhaling with relief as I shut the door behind me. Aside from the muted sounds of the crowd outside, the building was quiet.

At the foot of the stairs, I shuddered at the sight of the basement door sealed in crime-scene tape. As quietly as I could — I had no desire to get caught in conversation with Gabby or Mr. Benson or even Claire right now — I climbed to my aunt's apartment on the third floor and let myself in.

In the living room, I stared at my target: Aunt Emily's wall of travel photos. If I was right, one of these photos was not like the others.

After taking the postcards from my handbag, I started going through them one by one. The first postcard I selected showed the Great Pyramids of Egypt. On the travel wall, I found a photo of Emily on a camel, with the pyramids in the background. I moved to the second postcard, from Rio de Janeiro, and found a photo of Emily and Ted sunning themselves on the beach at Ipanema.

And so it went, postcard after postcard. The easy places with the recognizable landmarks — Paris, London, Moscow, Hong Kong, Rome, Athens, Cape Town, Beijing — were dealt with quickly. Postcards from places with buildings or geography I didn't recognize — Quito, Caracas, Dar es Salaam, Nairobi, Tel Aviv — took longer.

As I continued the process of matching postcards to photos, I realized that all of the photos on the wall featured Emily or Ted or both of them.

Except one. I stepped closer to it. The photo showed the Grand Canyon — a beautiful shot taken at sunset.

Frowning, I remembered something Emily had mentioned, seemingly in passing, a few years back: She'd regretted never visiting the Grand Canyon.

Look where I haven't been….

I removed the photo from the wall and flipped it over. The wood frame seemed perfectly ordinary. A bit chunky, perhaps, but nothing special.

Along the bottom edge of the frame, my finger caught a slight imperfection. I flipped it over. The imperfection was actually what looked like a rectangle carved into the wood, about the size of a lighter.

Except the rectangle wasn't a carving.

It was a cover.

I hurried to my handbag, pulled out a pair of tweezers, and gently pried the rectangular chunk of wood loose.

Revealed beneath, in a hollowed-out hiding spot, was a USB stick — the kind you insert into your computer to transfer files.

Pulse quickening, I removed the USB stick and held it up to the light, examining it from every angle.

It has no value, Emily had written. *But they won't know that. Use if needed.*

"You aren't making this easy, Aunt Emily," I said out loud. "Who is *they?*"

Without quite realizing what I'd already decided to do, I slipped the USB stick into my back pocket, fit the rectangular wood cover back into its slot on the frame, rehung the photo on the wall, and left my aunt's apartment.

On the second floor, I took a deep breath, my stomach fluttering with tension, and knocked on the door of the studio apartment.

I had no idea if Claire was even there, but I knew I had to see her right away. I needed to see her face.

I had to know for sure that she hadn't been involved in my aunt's death.

When the door opened, I took a deep breath and steeled myself.

Claire's eyes widened with concern. "Sarah, you're up and about. How are you feeling?"

"I'm fine."

She pulled me in for a hug. "I'm so glad you weren't seriously hurt."

I stepped back so I could see her face.

She sensed my mood. "What's wrong?"

"Aunt Emily was murdered," I blurted out.

"What do you mean?" she said sharply.

"She was run off the road."

She gasped quietly, then pulled me inside and shut the door.

"Tell me what you know," she said.

I told her what Matt had discovered. She listened intently, not saying a word.

When I finished, I took a deep breath. "But you already knew this, right?"

She shook her head. "We suspected, but no, we didn't know. We had no proof. Until now."

She started pacing back and forth in front of the bed, three steps one way, three steps the other, lost in thought.

Quietly, I slipped past her and took a seat at the small dining table. What Claire was doing was typical of her — she'd always preferred to move while thinking.

After a minute of pacing, she came to a decision and sat down. "Sarah, the information that Peter and Amy were tracking down ten years ago is still very dangerous."

"Even after all these years?"

"Even after all these years."

"Which means it's also still very valuable."

As we stared at each other, time seemed to slow. I was with someone I'd once known everything about. We'd shared every secret and adventure until life separated us and pushed us down divergent paths. In so many ways, the woman before me was a stranger. But deep inside, I knew —

"I have a new clue," I said before I could stop myself.

Claire blinked.

I pulled the second letter from my handbag and handed it to her.

She scanned it quickly, flipped it over, held it up to the light, then read it again before handing it back to me. "I assume you know what she's referring to."

"I do."

"What?"

"I found what she hid. It's a USB drive. In a picture frame upstairs."

"A picture frame?"

"Of the Grand Canyon. Emily traveled the world, but she never managed to make it there."

Claire returned her attention to the letter. "She says it has no value."

"I'm betting it's a decoy, a false clue, a fake."

I could almost see Claire's mind racing. "Maybe she found the real one and realized what it contained and destroyed it...."

"And replaced it, just in case someone came searching."

"She'd do that if she wanted to protect the information...."

"And didn't know who she could trust."

Claire sighed. "I'll need to analyze it."

"Of course. But first, I have to know."

"Know what?"

"Was Uncle Ted a spy?"

Claire went still. For a long moment, she didn't reply. Then her shoulders relaxed, just a fraction. "Yes."

"And Aunt Emily knew."

Her gaze held mine. I sensed turbulence within her, thoughts yearning to break free. "Spouses generally do."

Not always, I said to myself, flashing to what I hadn't known about my own lying husband. *At least not at first.*

I sighed. "Eventually, yes, they do."

"Eventually, all lies crumble."

"Do you really believe that?"

"I choose to believe that." She shook herself. "I choose to believe in a world in which today's secrets become tomorrow's history."

"Does that ever really happen?"

"It's supposed to happen, once the people involved can no longer be hurt and the secret has no present-day impact." Her lips tightened with frustration. "But in reality, it doesn't happen often enough. Secrecy for secrecy's sake is almost always a mistake."

"Not a sentiment I'd expect from a spy."

"Maybe I've become the Spy Who's Seen Too Much."

"Youthful idealism gone?"

"More often than not, people prove disappointing."

She went silent, her eyes shining with emotion. She'd missed me — I knew that deep inside, in my bones.

And I'd missed her, too.

For the first time in two decades, I was seeing my friend again. Not just a glimpse or a peek, but a full, uninterrupted exposure. Beneath that glamorous facade beat the same caring heart I'd known so well.

It was a heart that was bruised now. Older, wiser, sadder. But still beating.

Claire was still *Claire*.

"I'm sorry," I said, the words leaving my mouth before I could stop them.

"For what?" she said, going still.

"For letting you go," I said, swallowing back emotion. "For not fighting harder for our friendship. For falling into a new life in California and not giving you a way in. For letting my disappointment and anger and pride hold me back."

A tear rolled down her face. "Hold you back?"

"From reaching out and trying harder."

"Sarah," she said, her voice husky, "I'm the one who's sorry."

"It's okay. I get it now."

"No, you don't." She leaned across the table and took my hands in hers, gripping them tightly, her eyes filled with pain and regret. "There's so much I haven't shared."

It had been decades since I'd seen this Claire — vulnerable, open, uncertain.

"Claire, it's fine."

"No, it's not. It's not fine at all. I screwed this up. I screwed *us* up." She swallowed hard before fixing me with the fierce, determined expression I knew so well. "You were my best friend — my forever friend — and I pushed you away, deliberately, on purpose."

"Claire —"

"I convinced myself I was doing it to protect you. But I wasn't — I was doing it because I was selfish and full of myself. I believed my job made me special. I believed it made me better than everyone else, including you. I believed" — she laughed bitterly — "it was better to discard the past and embrace an enhanced future."

"An *enhanced* future?"

"Someone I worked for once used those very words."

"What does that even mean? Claire the robot super-soldier?"

That brought a smile. "If I told you, I'd have to kill you."

"Ha ha," I said. "But seriously, what does this all mean?"

"All too often, discarding the past means forgetting who you're protecting and why."

"Then let's be clear," I said, sitting up straighter. "I'm here for justice for Emily, Jerry, and your friend Peter."

She gave my hands a final squeeze and stood up. "Count me in. So let's get to it."

"How?" I said, rising with her.

"There's something you need to know." She was reaching for her handbag on the bed when her phone buzzed. She picked it up from the dresser, read the message, and went still.

"Sarah," she said after a short pause. "I have to go."

"What just happened?"

She gave me an anguished look. "I can't tell you."

My expression must have reflected my extreme disappointment, because without warning, she squared her shoulders and said, "No, screw that."

"Wait," I said, confused. "What's going on?"

"You're coming with me."

"I am?"

"You are." She looked me up and down, frowning. "We'll run by your house first."

"Why?"

"No offense? You're kind of a mess." She stepped closer to examine my neck. "We'll find something to cover the bruise."

"Why?"

She grabbed her handbag, no longer paying attention to me. "Okay, let's go."

I allowed her to usher me out the door, bewildered.

"Off we go," she said. "Chop, chop."

We flew down the stairs to the ground-floor hallway. I was about to open the entry door when I heard a knock.

I paused, uncertain what to do.

"See who it is," Claire said.

I pulled open the entry door and found Eddie the mailman standing on the sidewalk outside.

"Eddie," I said as a gust of cold air rushed over me. "Come in. What's up?"

Eddie frowned uncertainly at Claire and stepped into the hallway. I made quick introductions as I closed the door.

"Eddie," I said, "how did you know I was here?"

"Wendy told me."

"Wendy Danvers, from the *Gazette*?"

"She saw you come here."

"How do you know that?"

He stared at me, perplexed. "Because she told me."

"I mean, why did she tell you?"

"She asked about you."

"Why did she do that?"

"I have no idea," he said, exasperated. "How could I?"

I took a deep breath. "So why did you come here?"

"I figured out what was bugging me."

"About what?"

"About the handwriting."

I frowned, not following. "What handwriting?"

"On the delivery slip. It was the same."

"Wait," I said, confused. "What delivery are you talking about?"

He stared at me like I was daft, and maybe I was. "It was the same as Amy Messina's," he said impatiently.

That's when I got it. I glanced at Claire, who was listening intently. I felt my heart thump. "Amy Messina's signature was…."

"Distinctive. Not the usual scribble."

"And it reminded you of another signature? From someone else?"

"That's right." The frown I'd seen earlier was back. "Been bugging me all day."

"I'm sorry."

He shook his head. "Thought you should know." He checked his watch and turned to go. "Okay, gotta head. Route to finish."

"Wait, wait, wait," I said. "You didn't tell me whose signature it matched."

"It wasn't a match," he said irritably. "The

names are different."

"But the handwriting…."

"Oh, sure. The handwriting is the same."

It took every ounce of willpower not to grab him and shake the information loose. "Whose handwriting did it match, Eddie?"

His eyes widened. He was gazing past me. "Hers."

That's when I heard it: a soft *phffft*.

Next to me, Claire cried out in surprise.

As I turned toward her, she let out a soft sigh and, without warning, collapsed against me.

"Claire!" I said frantically, barely managing to prevent her — and me — from falling to the floor.

As gently as I could, I laid her down.

Her eyes rolled back in her head, then closed.

"Claire," I said, "wake up!"

What had just happened?

I felt for a pulse — yes, it was there.

Then I froze as my fingers touched —

What was that?

I turned her head to the side and found —

A dart!

In her neck!

"She's not dead," I heard a voice say.

I whirled around.

Hialeah Truegood stood ten feet away, a gun in her hand and a smirk on her face.

"But she will be if you don't do what I say."

CHAPTER 28

The Southern accent was gone. The outer shell of Hialeah Truegood — the thick tumble of red hair, the expertly applied makeup, the gorgeous full-length skirt — remained intact, but her essence had changed. There was a hardness in this woman's gaze, a cold intelligence, a sense of triumph.

The woman in front of me was a *disguise*, I realized.

Hiding the one-and-only Amy Messina, who was very much *not* dead.

"Here's what's going to happen," Amy said to me and Eddie, her voice controlled and steady. "The two of you are going to pick up Claire and carry her into the basement."

Fear stabbed through me.

"*Now.*"

Eddie seemed stunned, unable to tear his gaze from the gun aimed at us.

"Eddie," I said, "we need to do what she says."

Eddie blinked. "What?"

"Pick up her legs. I'll get her shoulders."

As unobtrusively as I could, I plucked the dart from Claire's neck and set it on the floor.

Eddie and I carried Claire down the hallway. Amy was careful to keep a distance between herself and us, perhaps to guard against me or Eddie lunging at her. I silently cursed when she retrieved the dart from the hallway floor and slipped it into a skirt pocket.

When we reached the basement door, Amy said, "Pull off the crime scene tape and drop it. Then carry her down."

I removed the tape, reluctantly letting it go, and pushed open the basement door, which creaked as it revealed the darkness below. After flipping on the light switch, I said to Eddie, "Ready?"

Slowly, we maneuvered Claire down the steps, the stairs groaning under our combined weight.

"Put her there," Amy said, pointing to a spot on the ground in the middle of the basement.

The same spot where poor Jerry had died.

"You won't get away with this," I said as we laid Claire down.

Amy didn't reply. For a long second, she stood

silently at the foot of the stairs, ten feet away, the gun aimed right at us.

"You and I," she said to me. "We need to talk."

"Of course, Amy. We can talk all you want."

"Amy?" she repeated. "That disguise died a long time ago." She swung her attention to Eddie. "Hey, Mr. Mailman. What's your name?"

"Eddie," he said. "Eddie Jones."

"Move a little closer, Eddie Jones."

He stepped forward.

"One more step, Eddie Jones."

As he did so, Amy pressed the trigger and — with a soft *phffft* — shot a dart into his neck.

He collapsed with a surprised groan.

"Eddie!" I cried as I rushed toward him, barely managing to slow his fall before he hit the ground next to Claire.

I knelt at his side, tears threatening. His head lolled back — he was already out cold. Angrily, I glared up at our captor. "What's wrong with you?"

That got a smile. "Finally, some spirit."

"What do you want?"

"That's what I've been considering." She gestured to the hole in the wall. "What do you know about laying bricks?"

I tried to avoid glancing at the hole, which was still gaping at me. On the ground next to Claire was the stuff I'd helped Jerry carry down — replacement bricks, bags of sand and cement mix, water buckets, a mixing tub, a trowel — right where he'd left it.

"Not much," I said cautiously.

"Don't be modest. You're pretty handy — I noticed that in the cafe. A real Ms. Fixer-Upper." She gestured to the bricks. "So get started."

"Get started what?"

"I want you to brick up the hole in the wall."

I stared at her, not following. "You want me to fill in the hole?"

She nodded, waiting for me to catch up.

"If I don't?"

"Then I'll shoot you."

She was serious — I knew that without question.

I had to do something — but what? Could I distract her? Slow her down?

"I don't see why you want me to do that," I said, trying to buy time.

"Don't overthink this, Sarah. You just need to do what I want you to do." She waved the gun. "Decision time. Help or die?"

"Help," I said. "I'll help you fill in the hole."

"Good. Quietly, please. My trigger finger is allergic to noise."

I gestured to a bucket. "I'll need water."

She stepped to the sink on the opposite wall, examined the area, then returned to her spot at the foot of the stairs. "That's fine. Remember what happens if you misbehave."

Still on my knees, I inched closer to a bag of cement mix and began reading the instructions. "Is this how it went with Peter?"

"Focus on the hole, Sarah."

"I don't know anything about the information you were after a decade ago, but clearly it was valuable enough to kill for." When she didn't object, I continued. "You managed to get your hands on some but not all of it, didn't you?"

She gave me a sad smile. "Is this the moment where I'm supposed to reveal my diabolical master plan?"

Yes, I almost said, *that would be great.* Instead, I said, "Rather than give the information back to your agency, you saw an opportunity to profit from it."

When she didn't respond, I pressed on.

"But something went wrong, and Peter discovered your plan. So you had to silence him."

"Quite the storyteller," she murmured.

"After a decade away, what brought you back to Eagle Cove? Did you run out of money? Did you decide to come back to search for the rest of the information so you could sell it, too?"

She wasn't going to answer me, I realized, but at least she was no longer objecting to my fumblings.

"You reached out to Emily again, didn't you?" I asked, taking a stab in the dark.

She went still, just for a second, and I knew I'd guessed right.

"Something you said or did raised her suspicions."

Her lips tightened.

"She didn't have a car crash on her own, did she?"

That got a response. "I'm curious what the sheriff found when he recovered her car."

"Car paint on the side — from another car."

"So he put two and two together."

"He doesn't know about you, in case you're wondering," I said, suddenly worried she'd go after Matt after finishing with me. "He doesn't know a thing about this spy stuff."

That drew a snort. "Is that how you think about this? Spy *stuff*?"

"What else am I supposed to think?"

She waved the gun. "As entertaining as this is, I need you to focus on the job at hand."

"Fine." I tore open the bag of cement mix. "The instructions say I need to mix one part cement with four parts sand."

She watched as I poured the cement powder into the mixing tub, followed by a much larger bag of sand.

I looked at my dusty hands and grimaced.

"I have to mix the cement and sand together before I add the water," I said. "I need a shovel."

"I don't see one," she said, scanning the basement, then pointed to the sledgehammer — the very tool I'd used to bash in the wall — on the floor nearby. "You'll have to make do with that."

I reached for the sledgehammer, trying not to appear too eager. The hammer wasn't designed for mixing, but I didn't care, because maybe I could —

"Remember my finger on this trigger," she said, anticipating my thoughts. "You swing, I shoot."

I gripped the smooth wooden handle tight with frustration. Still on my knees, I pushed the end of the sledgehammer into the sand and cement in the tub and started mixing.

After a minute of concentrated effort in which not a single helpful idea made it into my head, I set the sledgehammer down and got to my feet, sweating and breathing hard.

"Ready to add water," I said, then picked up a bucket, skirted past the unconscious pair to the sink on the opposite wall, and positioned the bucket under the faucet. I turned on the tap and water rushed in, the sudden roar echoing in the silence.

To my left, I noticed the dumbwaiter shaft, its door partially open for Mr. Snuggles's benefit, and recalled what Gabby had said: *Sounds carry.*

My heart quickened. I'd found my glimmer of hope — and now I had to run with it.

"So, Amy," I said loudly after shutting off the tap. I pretended to struggle as I wrestled the bucket out of the sink. "Jerry Meachum recognized you, didn't he?"

"Jerry," Amy said dismissively. "One of those rare people who actually notice things."

Anger surged through me. "That day in the cafe, he recognized you beneath that ridiculous disguise, didn't he? So before he could tell anyone who you really were, you sat him down for a reading and told him a story — something to keep him quiet until you could deal with him."

She didn't reply, her attention fixed on me like I was a problem she was deciding how to solve.

"Why not me, too?" I said. "When I found Jerry in the basement, I nearly found you as well."

"One of those words is your answer."

I realized she meant "nearly" and shivered. How close to death I'd come. If I'd caught sight of her, I wouldn't be here now....

"What I still don't understand," I said, "is how, ten years ago, you convinced Aunt Emily to cover up your murder of Peter and hide his body. What lie did you use?"

Though Amy didn't reply, a sad smile appeared on her face.

"Was it the lie about you running away from an abusive husband?" I said, as much to myself as to her. "No, that's not right. That lie was the one you came up with for Gabby and Mr. Benson."

Again, I sensed her interest quickening. My guesses weren't off target. She was curious what I'd figured out.

It was then, like the proverbial bolt from the blue, that I saw it. I inhaled sharply. "Emily knew you were an agent."

Amy smiled with approval. "Brava."

"Which means…."

And suddenly, just like that, *I knew*.

I couldn't breathe.

It was like a bomb going off in my head. For the first time, I saw the light.

I understood what Claire had almost shared upstairs.

The truth had been staring me in the face all along, waiting for me to appreciate it.

Emily's years abroad with Uncle Ted….

The postcards she'd mailed me from exotic spots across the globe….

Her ability to organize a sting operation with law enforcement….

Her knowledge of how to handle a corpse….

Her carefully planned, cryptic notes….

Her ability to replace a flash drive with a convincing fake….

Uncle Ted wasn't the only secret agent in the family.

I couldn't restrain a gasp. "Emily was one of you."

"Brava," Amy said.

"My aunt was a spy!"

"Retired, but yes."

"She was someone your agency trusted."

A smile flitted across Amy's lips.

"You came to her as an agent in trouble."

When it became clear she wasn't going to answer, I continued. "Somehow, you convinced her to not tell anyone, including the agency." More silence. "You told her a story, and she bought it."

"I see some of her in you," Amy said. She appeared to be enjoying my fumbling quest for the truth — so I kept on.

"Maybe the story was that you couldn't trust anyone at the agency. Maybe you told her the agency had been infiltrated and you were on a mole hunt or some such."

"A mole hunt?" Amy said, amused.

"I don't know the lingo. All I know about spies is from books and movies and TV. But yes, you told her something that made her decide to take you in. Something that made her decide to hide the body in the basement rather than tell your agency about it."

"That's actually not far from the truth. Congratulations."

"Thank you."

"You might as well know," Amy said. "Your aunt was a legend."

"A legend?" I repeated, stunned.

"All the young agents looked up to her. Especially the women. She was a trailblazer."

Out of the corner of my eye, I sensed movement. Was Claire coming to? I didn't dare peek, so I picked up the bucket of water and started carrying it to the cement mixing tub.

"Ow," I said loudly. I set the bucket down next to Claire, sending water sloshing to the floor.

"What are you doing?" Amy said.

"Sorry, back spasm," I said, bending lower. From this angle, Amy couldn't see my face. She also couldn't see Claire's face.

Which meant she couldn't see what I saw: *Claire was awake.* For one long second, our eyes locked onto each other.

Impatiently, Amy said, "Sarah, you're no good to me if you can't do the work."

"Sorry," I said, grimacing with pretend-pain as I slowly straightened. "It's just something that happens sometimes. It'll pass." Carefully, I grabbed the bucket handle and faux-struggled to carry it the final few feet to the mixing tub.

When I glanced at Amy, I saw a speculative expression, like she was trying to make up her mind about something.

"What?" I said.

"It's time to hand over the USB stick."

I froze. "What stick?"

"The one in your back pocket."

My mind started racing. "I only just found that. How could you…?"

She smirked but didn't answer.

"You put a camera in my aunt's apartment," I said slowly. "You saw me take down the photo and find the USB stick in the picture frame."

"Good," she said approvingly. "I'm curious: What was the deal with the postcards?"

"The postcards?"

"The ones you kept referencing while you searched."

"They helped me figure out the clue."

"What clue?"

I told her about Emily's second letter, leaving out the part about the USB stick having no value.

Amy frowned, puzzled. "What did she mean, 'Look where I haven't been?'"

"When I was a kid, Emily sent me postcards from every exotic place she visited."

"And?"

"In her apartment, she had a wall of photos of her and Uncle Ted from their world travels. I realized Emily was pointing me to a photo of a place she *hadn't* been."

"And that place was…."

"The Grand Canyon."

Amy smiled approvingly. "Good job, Sarah."

I took the USB stick from my back pocket and tossed it to her. It landed on the ground at her feet.

"Weak throw, Sarah," Amy said. "Very weak."

"Sorry. It's just with my back…."

"I'm pretty sure your back is fine, Sarah. Regardless, I hope that poor back of yours isn't going to prevent you from doing what I asked."

"The back's for real, but yes, I can still fix the wall." Faux-gingerly, I picked up the bucket and poured the water into the mixing tub, then got down on my knees and picked up the hand trowel.

"No funny business with that tool in your hands."

For a moment I didn't reply, focusing instead on using the trowel to mix sand and cement into the water. Then I said, "Amy, I still don't understand how you can do this to someone you worked with."

"If you worked with the people I worked with, you'd understand."

"Claire's my friend. She isn't a bad person."

Amy sighed. "You are so naive."

I risked a glance at Claire and saw her gaze dart from the trowel, to my face, and then back to the trowel.

Okay, I could work with that.

In the mixing tub, the mortar was thickening. I scooped some onto the trowel and held it up to show Amy. "I'll need more water. I still don't get why you want me to fill in the hole."

"The hole is part of the story," Amy said.

"What do you mean, the story?"

"Your story. A sad tale of accidental murder, followed by suicide."

I tried to ignore the stab of fear. "That'll never fly."

"Really?" She cocked her head, considering. "It just might, given the physical evidence."

"What physical evidence?"

She smirked and pointed to my hands, now covered in sand and cement. I swallowed as I realized what her plan was.

"Here's how the story will go," she said. "Ready?"

I set the mortar-laden trowel on the ground between me and Claire. "Whatever it is, it won't work."

"I think it will." She was enjoying herself, I realized. Back in the day, she'd probably been a natural at giving presentations. "After all, you and Claire were once great friends, until you had a falling out. It won't take much to convince people you got into an argument that escalated and led to you killing her and Eddie."

"Nonsense," I said.

"With local cops, the obvious answer is usually

good enough. In this case, the obvious answer is you."

"Me?"

"You're the central player in everything that happened here. You knocked in the hole. You found Jerry. Who else but you?"

I stared at her, speechless.

"The more I think about this story, the more I see the possibilities." The smirk returned. "Who knows? Maybe you were also here ten years ago. Maybe you killed Peter Messina and good old Aunt Emily covered up for *you*."

"Wait…."

"And then, ten years later, you shot and killed Jerry because he noticed something."

"But I was shot, too."

"Ah, but you weren't. After killing Jerry, you hid the gun, then jabbed yourself with a dart. Voila, instant alibi."

I shook my head, trying to follow.

"When you asked your old friend Claire to help you cover it up, she objected, so you shot her in the hallway. Eddie saw it happen, so you forced him to help you carry Claire down here and then you shot him, too. You decided to bury the bodies behind the wall and started mixing the mortar. But then you realized you couldn't hope to cover this up. Or maybe you realized you didn't want to."

I shook my head. This woman was so twisted. "No one will ever buy that."

"Once they analyze the physical evidence, they may have no choice. It's your fingerprints on the crime-scene tape, your fingerprints on the tools down here, your hands covered in cement mix...."

I had to keep her talking. "How does this crazy story end?"

"As a pointless tragedy, of course. Overcome with remorse about your ill-considered actions and despondent over your failed life, you decided to end it all."

"My failed life?" I whispered.

"I'll grant you the daughter," Amy said. "She turned out fine. As for the rest — how sad."

To my surprise, the words stung. "I don't agree."

"Oh?" she said with a sneer, her calm demeanor slipping away. "You're a sad, lonely, divorced, middle-aged failure, recently laid off, no job prospects, no direction, living alone in a house that reminds you of your crooked ex." She shook her head with contempt. "Your life is so empty, you let a small-town mayor manipulate you into offering up your time and labor, free of charge, for a stupid tourist event. Need I go on?"

"You're not really talking about me, are you?" I said quietly.

She cocked her head, not following.

"You're talking about yourself."

She let out a contemptuous snort. "Sarah Boone, armchair psychologist."

"But I'm right, aren't I?" I said, pressing on, my voice rising. "Those fears are yours, not mine. When you consider your life — your sad, lonely, anxious life — you hate what you see. Constantly looking over your shoulder, haunted by your past, hiding behind ridiculous disguises, unable to show anyone who you truly are."

She flushed. "Back to the mortar."

"You probably thought you could reinvent yourself and buy a happy life with the information you stole. But that's not how it worked out, is it? At the end of the day, you're desperately alone, aren't you? No one to share your worries with, no one who knows the real you — and by *you* I mean murderer of a bunch of people for financial gain. No decent person would ever want a greedy killer like you in their life."

From across the basement, I heard a faint scratching sound and couldn't stop myself from glancing over. I let out a small gasp as Mr. Snuggles emerged from the dumbwaiter shaft and hopped to the ground. He looked at me and then Amy, sniffing the air and getting his bearings.

"Aww, the local kitty cat," Amy sneered. "Here to catch a rat?"

Mr. Snuggles hissed at her, clearly not a fan.

And that's when the world sped up.

Without warning, Claire grabbed the trowel and flung wet mortar at Amy, splattering her face and dress with cement.

Amy whirled toward Claire, the gun swinging away from me.

I grabbed the sledgehammer and ran forward, ramming the wooden handle into Amy's stomach.

Amy cried out in surprise and pain, her gun arm dropping —

And I tackled her.

I had no idea what I was doing — no plan of action, no experience, no training beyond beginner kung fu — but holy mother of all that was good and true, a wave of fury and rage and frustration and grief rushed through me and —

Screaming like a banshee, arms flailing, I tore into her, punching and scratching my way into eternity.

She tried to swing the gun around —

But the force of my body against hers sent us flying —

Onto the floor.

Where her head hit the cement floor —

And with a groan, she lost consciousness.

Gasping for breath, I jumped off of her and stared down at her silent form with disbelief.

I'd fought her — and won?

Exhilaration roared through me, my heart racing, my lungs fighting for breath.

Yes, I'd won!

There was a clatter on the stairs and Gabby charged down, cane at the ready, Mr. Benson at her heels.

"You get her, Sarah?"

"Got her," I gasped.

"Sheriff's on the way."

Mr. Benson pointed to the dumbwaiter door. "Message received, loud and clear."

Mr. Snuggles hissed again at Amy, then dashed to Mr. Benson and leaped into his arms.

Claire crawled to the gun, knocking it away from Amy. "Good job, Sarah."

Relief rushed through me — relief and so much more. Raising my arms high, I let loose a cry of release that felt like it had been years in coming.

Gabby stepped closer and prodded Amy's unconscious form with her cane. "Some psychic you are," she sniffed, then leaned over her and yelled, "Didn't see *this* coming, didja?"

CHAPTER 29

The following morning, long after Amy was hauled away handcuffed to a stretcher, long after Claire and Eddie and I were carefully examined and cleared by Doc Barnes, long after Matt and his deputies asked us questions for hours, and long after Mom was finally allowed to take me and Claire home for some good old-fashioned (and very welcome) maternal smothering, I called the gang and told them to meet us at the cafe for a debrief.

Bright sunlight streamed through the storefront windows as Mom and Claire and I pushed open the cafe door and stepped inside, the lovely aromas of hot coffee and freshly baked muffins bidding us welcome. Janie was already there, bustling about in the kitchen. Gabby and Mr. Benson came down moments later, Mr. Snuggles not far behind.

It was funny thinking of this motley band of misfits as my gang, yet that's exactly what they were. More than that: They were my *friends*. I couldn't imagine the past two weeks without them.

At the house earlier that morning, while Mom was downstairs fixing us a big breakfast, Claire and I had worked through what we could and couldn't share, trying to anticipate the questions that would come up and the answers we'd need to give.

"They'll figure it out eventually," I'd warned her.

"Not if you play your part," she'd said.

Mr. Benson, Gabby, Janie and my mom settled into a table at the front window, clearly impatient to learn all.

"You girls get over here!" Gabby ordered me and Claire. "We need the skinny."

Claire and I exchanged smiles and pulled up chairs.

Mr. Snuggles eyed my lap and, deciding that was where he wanted to be, hopped gracefully onto my legs and settled in, gazing up at me contentedly.

"What we tell you has to stay with us," I said solemnly, reassured by the throaty purring of the adorable cat in my lap. "No sharing."

"Of course," Mr. Benson said, the others nodding quick assent.

I had no illusions about their discretion — no one at that table was truly capable of keeping her or his mouth shut — but Claire had suggested I say it. "If you tell them you're sharing a secret," she'd said, "they're more likely to believe you."

Claire and I had already decided I should take the lead, so I sat up straight and cleared my throat. "Okay, gang. Here's what happened in the basement with Amy." I laid out the action in full, sparing no details about the ambush on the stairs, Amy's instructions for me to start fixing the wall, and the life-and-death struggle on the basement floor.

"What in the world was that lunatic up to?" Gabby said.

"Honestly, I have no idea." A total lie, of course, but one that was necessary to keep Claire's spy job out of the picture.

"Clearly," Mr. Benson said, "that young woman misrepresented herself a decade ago."

"I've been told this in confidence, so you can't share this," I said, knowing full well that what I was about to say would be disseminated at lightning speed to every nook and cranny of the Eagle Cove gossip network. "Peter and Amy had criminal records in multiple states for passing bad checks, identity theft, and more."

Mr. Benson inhaled sharply. "They were con artists?"

"Apparently," I said.

"Then...." It took him a few seconds to

organize his thoughts. "What else was a lie? Was Peter really a wife-beater?"

"We don't know. Quite possibly he wasn't."

Gabby was frowning. "The whole thing was a con?"

"Apparently."

Her voice rose in outrage. "That mousy little wretch put one over on me?"

Mr. Benson was shaking his head. "I must say, I find it hard to believe that Amy could have fooled Emily. Emily had an infallible nose for the truth. Nothing ever got past her."

"Unfortunately," I said, "no one is infallible."

Mr. Benson sat upright as an idea hit him. "What else is a lie?"

"What do you mean?" I asked.

"Did Emily actually kill Peter?"

Gabby swiveled toward him. "You're saying Amy — not Emily— killed Peter, and Emily decided to cover for Amy and take the fall?"

I held my breath, hoping they'd continue down this speculative path.

Janie shifted in her seat. "If Amy killed him, that means Emily isn't a murderer."

"Oh, Janie," Mom threw in, "I like the sound of that."

Gabby was frowning. "Why would Emily cover for her like that?"

I tried to sound uncertain. "Maybe Emily really

did know Amy's parents. Then Amy showed up here, bruised and bleeding, with a story about an abusive marriage. Let's say Emily believed her. What would Emily have done?"

"If we accept your premise," Mr. Benson said slowly, "then Emily's instinct would have been to help her."

Gabby looked at Mr. Benson skeptically but remained silent.

"Remember," I added, "Amy's a con artist. A skillful one. When it comes to fooling people, she's a professional."

Gabby shook her head, not satisfied. "Why did that wretch come back here after all these years? She got away with murder. Emily's letter said Amy wasn't involved at all. The cops and D.A. couldn't do a thing to her."

I tried to appear unconcerned. "I wish I had the answers."

"Was she after something?" Gabby continued. "Something she'd left behind? Something she forgot?" Her frown deepened. "Maybe Emily had something here all these years and didn't realize it? Something Amy wanted or was afraid of?"

"All good questions," I said. "But I have no idea. If I had to guess, maybe money? Maybe she thought Peter had hidden money here years ago, so she came back to find it? Maybe we'll find out at the trial?"

Gabby was still chewing. "Why a dart gun? I can see her using a real gun. But a dart gun with a tranquilizer — who has one of those? What was she, an elephant trainer?"

"Apparently she'd had the dart gun for a while," I said. "The puncture marks on my neck and Jerry Meachum's neck matched the mark on Peter Messina's neck."

Janie breathed in sharply. "On *Peter's* neck? They could tell that, even after all these years?"

"When Aunt Emily dried out the body, the puncture mark on the skin was preserved."

Mom shivered. "I can't believe Emily helped that terrible woman. Right here in this building."

"I should have seen through it," Gabby said darkly. "Then and now. All that fortune-telling nonsense."

"That disguise part of it, I think I understand," I said cautiously. "Amy wanted to make sure no one recognized her when she came back, so she took on a very different persona."

Gabby harrumphed, clearly not satisfied.

I added, "Pretending to be a real person was a smart move."

"Why do you say that?" Mr. Benson asked.

"Because a real person has a real history. So if anyone checks...."

"I see," he said slowly. "Hiding in plain sight."

"Exactly."

"I must admit, the disguise worked on me. Not once did I make the connection."

Gabby snorted. "Fooling you is easy, old man."

"Woman, when will you stop —"

"Sarah," Mom said, jumping in. "What does Matthew say about all this?"

"The prosecutor told him the evidence is a slam dunk. With the dart gun, the marks on Jerry's and Peter's necks, and testimony from me and Claire and Eddie, Amy will be in jail for a very long time."

Mom shuddered. "Poor Jerry."

Janie said, "He recognized her, didn't he? Here in the cafe that day?"

"Unfortunately," I said.

"And that's why Amy…."

"Yep."

"Poor kid didn't stand a chance," Gabby said.

The table went silent. We had a memorial service to attend that afternoon — one that would be difficult for all of us.

"Well," Mom finally said. "I'm glad she's behind bars."

"Amen to that."

"I hope she stays there forever."

Gabby turned to Claire. "You've been quiet."

Claire gave her a wan smile. "Still not feeling a hundred percent, to be honest." Indeed, she seemed tired — understandably so, after being shot full of horse tranquilizer. But I also sensed a certain wistfulness. She was enjoying the back-and-forth but knew she would soon be leaving it behind.

Janie said, "Can I get you something? A cup of coffee? A muffin?"

Claire smiled. "I'm good, Janie, thanks."

Mr. Benson said, "After you rest up, what are your plans, young lady?"

Claire said, "I'm heading back to D.C." She said it brightly, but I sensed she wasn't as enthused as she seemed.

"It's been nice having you here, even if only briefly. Promise you'll visit soon."

"I promise I will." Her expression was shy. "In fact, if it's okay with you all, I'd love to come up for Christmas."

"Of course!" I said, pleased. "Anna and I will be here, too."

"Claire, you're more than welcome to stay with me and Ed," Janie said.

"Or with us," Mom added.

Claire smiled with gratitude. "Thank you. It's been too long. The truth is, I've missed you. All of you."

Mom reached over and squeezed her hand. "Exactly what I wanted to hear."

Gabby turned toward me. "What about you, Sarah? What are your plans?"

I took a deep breath. I'd been expecting the question. And until that moment, I thought I'd known the answer. But as my mouth opened, it hit me — *I was wrong.* For several days now, a realization had been sneaking up on me, bubbling beneath the surface of my conscious mind, not quite ready to pop forth.

Until now.

I swallowed back a wave of emotion as the ramifications of my decision — *Was I really doing this?* — rose before me.

I felt my cheeks flushing pink. My heart picked up its pace, beating faster and faster.

Six pairs of eyes were fixed on me, keenly interested in what I was about to say.

I cleared my throat, trying to calm down. "I have a question for Janie."

"For me?" Janie said, surprised.

I tried to keep my voice from trembling. "How would you like to become business partners?"

Janie breathed in sharply. "Business partners? To do what?"

"To re-open the cafe. Permanently, you and me. You handle the menu, I handle the operations. Equal partners."

Aside from Mom's gasp, the room had gone completely quiet.

As one, the table's attention swung to Janie, who blinked and stared at me, clearly stunned.

Then, unable to contain herself, she let out a yell of pure joy.

"Yes!"

The cafe erupted in a round of cheering and laughing.

"Sarah," my mom said, reaching over to grip my hands. "Does this mean you're staying?"

"Yes, Mom," I said as tears welled up. "It means I'm staying."

"Hurray!" she said, the others joining in.

"I'll be moving into Aunt Emily's apartment on the third floor," I said to Gabby and Mr. Benson. "Which means we'll be getting to know each other very well."

Everyone was so caught up in the cheering and laughter that no one heard the chime of the cafe door opening. A gust of cold air alerted me.

When I glanced at the door, I froze.

A gasp left my throat.

Heads whirled.

Claire leaped to her feet, ready to attack.

Gabby yelled, "Jail break!"

Amy Messina stood at the door in her fortune-teller outfit, frozen with surprise.

I could barely breathe.

But wait.

Something was off.

I squinted at her, zeroing in on little details.

It wasn't Amy.

There were subtle differences. The hair and clothes and makeup were the same — scarily so — but this woman's nose was slightly longer, her mouth slightly wider.

The eyes were the same vivid green, but they weren't the same eyes. The personality flowing from them felt very different.

"I'm so sorry to intrude," the woman said, her voice breathy and eerily familiar. "I can come back later if you all would prefer." The lush Southern accent, the soft whispery tone, the apologetic gestures — all of it, truly uncanny.

Gabby leaned closer. "You're not her, are you?"

The woman inhaled sharply. "I'm not who?"

"I'm sorry," I said, standing up and feeling very awkward. "I'm Sarah Boone, the owner of this cafe." As the words left my mouth, I realized how much I liked the way they sounded. "And you are?"

"My name is Hialeah Truegood," the woman said.

Her announcement was greeted with stunned silence.

It really wasn't Amy beneath the makeup — I knew that now — but why would the real Hialeah Truegood show up *here*? I realized my mouth was hanging open, so I shut it, unsure what to say.

Hialeah inched back toward the door. "I apologize. I've intruded on a private moment."

"No, please, it's fine," I said. "It's just…. You

remind us of someone." I arranged a smile on my face. "Is there something I can help you with?"

Hialeah hesitated, even as her gaze wandered avidly over the cafe. "I'm afraid I won't be able to explain. I don't fully understand it myself."

"Explain what?" I asked.

"Why I'm here." She paused, collecting her thoughts. "You see, I've been drawn here."

"Drawn here?"

"By the spirits."

You could have heard a pin drop. Okay, this was beyond odd. Although after the events of the past two weeks, perhaps it was time to adjust my understanding of "odd."

Mr. Benson cleared his throat. "The spirits, my dear?"

"Indeed." A warm smile lit up her face as she took him in. "Oh, kind sir, you have a lovely aura. I'm a medium, you see, blessed with the ability to communicate with the spirit world."

Mr. Benson's face flushed. The others, still astonished, seemed unable to do anything but stare.

I cleared my throat. "And you say you were drawn here, Ms. Truegood?"

"I've been having dreams — recurring dreams — of myself in a new place. A place I've never been. With people I've never met. A place so unlike my native New Orleans."

"And that place is…?"

She took a deep breath. "When I saw leaves in lovely shades of orange and red, I packed my bags and got in my car and drove north. I saw a lake, shimmering and beautiful. And an eagle, soaring in the bright blue sky. And a kind woman baking treats with love and care."

Janie let out a gasp.

I swallowed back a rush of emotion. "And somehow, those images brought you here?"

"My help will be needed here," Hialeah said solemnly. "It's rare for the spirits to be this clear. And insistent! Though part of what they shared, I must confess, confuses me."

"Confuses you?"

"In my visions, I'm bearing witness — aware of what is happening, yet not part of it." She frowned. "In the visions, I'm not me. I can see me, but the me I see is not me."

I shot a glance at Claire, who shrugged as if to say, *This is a new one for me.*

Hialeah sounded apologetic. "I know this must be confusing."

"Not as confusing as you might think," I said slowly.

Hialeah leaned closer, examining my face, clearly puzzled. "Have we met?"

"Not exactly," I said. "I mean, no."

"You've seen it, too, haven't you?" she said. "No, wait, you haven't." She took a deep breath, then surprised me by reaching out and taking my hands in hers.

Her grip was firm, almost painfully tight.

"But you will," she said. "In time, Sarah Boone, you will see it all."

CHAPTER 30

The following morning, after a night of restful and much-needed sleep, I awoke in my childhood bedroom to find sunlight flooding through the windows and Claire already up and out of the house.

On my phone was a text from her: "Free at noon for an afternoon drive?"

I resisted the urge to ask if "an afternoon drive" was code for "more secret spy stuff" and typed back my agreement. After getting showered and dressed and fed, I made my way to the front porch to await her arrival. The midday sun felt warm on my cheeks, the air carrying the familiar scent of fallen leaves.

I heard an engine and, covering my eyes against the sun, watched Matt's truck round the corner. He parked in front and made his way toward me, a grin on his face.

"Hey, you," I said, ignoring the flutter of undeniable attraction. Head to toe, this sheriff thing of his *worked*. "What brings you here?"

"Wanted to check on you." He stepped onto the porch and joined in facing the midday sun. "So how are you?"

"Good. I slept like a log."

"Claire around?"

"She went out earlier, but she's on her way back."

"You two have plans?"

"She wants to take a drive."

"How's she feeling? Any after-effects from the dart?"

"She's fine, I think."

"When is she heading back to D.C.?"

"Tomorrow. But she's promised to visit more often. And keep in touch."

"What about you? What are your immediate plans?"

We turned toward each other. After my big revelation the previous day, I'd made three phone calls — to my daughter, my sister, and Matt, in that order — and told them what I'd decided to do.

"Still working that out. I'm flying back to California in two days to begin packing up the house."

"You selling it?"

"That's the idea."

"How did Anna take the news?"

"She's happy for me, I think, and excited about visiting the East Coast and spending more time with Mom and Grace and her cousins. She's already talking about summer road trips to Boston and New York."

"Any sense of when you'll reopen the cafe?"

"Not yet. Janie and I have a lot of work ahead of us. We might do another 'pop-up' over the holidays — baked goods only — and expand the menu early next year."

"Hot meals?"

"That's the plan. Breakfast and lunch."

"The town will welcome you with open arms."

I grinned. "Glad to hear."

"So," he said. "A serious question."

"Sure."

"You've been through a lot in the past two weeks." His gaze intensified. "Really and truly, how are you?"

I thought about his question for a moment. "The past two weeks have been a rollercoaster. Grief, shock, fear, anger over what Amy did to poor Jerry — the works. But right now, at this moment, what I feel most is *relief.*"

I saw sympathy and understanding in his eyes as he waited for me to continue.

"I'm relieved it's over. Relieved we know what really happened. Relieved it didn't end up even worse." I took a deep breath. "Claire and Eddie and I survived. Aunt Emily didn't actually murder anyone. Amy is behind bars and will stay there for a very long time."

His shoulders tensed. "About that."

"What?" I said warily.

"The Feds swooped in this morning and took custody of her."

I breathed in sharply. I'd been expecting this — Amy's spy agency doubtless had questions for her — but the news was still a jolt. "What does that mean?"

"We'll see."

"Where'd they take her?"

"D.C."

"I assume she'll be brought back to stand trial for Jerry's murder?"

"Not if she pleads out." His expression flashed with emotion. "What I said before about being careful? It still applies."

I frowned. "Why do you say that?"

He didn't answer right away. His jaw was clenching again, which meant he was once again debating the pros and cons of sharing information with me.

He knows there's more to this, I realized.

"Because...." He searched my face intently, like

he was trying to figure out if I knew anything. "I just want you to be careful."

"Why do I need to be careful?"

"In the past four days, you tangled with a killer twice."

"The killer's caught. Problem solved, right?"

He didn't reply, and his gaze never left me as he tried to decide how best to handle a certain vexatious problem named Sarah Boone.

I could have let him off the hook at that point — I sensed he was willing to move to a different topic — but I couldn't stop myself. "Or are you saying there's more?"

After more silence, he exhaled slowly, as if accepting the inevitability of him choosing to confide in me. "Remember how fast we got the DNA match for Peter Messina?"

I nodded, waiting for him to continue.

"Matches *never* come that fast."

"Meaning what?"

"On its own, nothing."

"You're building to something."

Now that he'd committed to sharing, his voice took on a determined edge. "Peter Messina's background. A high school graduate who worked at a paper mill. Lived in New Hampshire his entire life. No police record prior to his wife filing a report for domestic violence."

"Which means?"

"Amy's background, same thing. Went to the same high school as Peter, three years behind him, worked in retail in the same area as Peter's paper mill, no police record."

He was laying out his case in an oblique manner. Explaining without explaining. Handing me pieces of the puzzle and expecting me to fit them together.

"What are you saying?"

"Why were his palms burned?"

I blinked, taken aback.

"You said it yourself, right here on this porch. Why burn his palms? There's nothing in his background that explains why that would be necessary for *him*."

I knew why, of course. When Claire's spy agency had invented Peter's fake background, they hadn't known about his burned palms. So his fake background hadn't included anything to explain them.

"More to the point," he continued. "Why did Amy and Emily do that?"

"It had to be Amy," I said.

It was both of them and you know it, his expression told me. But what his mouth said was, "That Amy is one cool customer. Not a single word spoken in custody. Not a single phone call. But watching everything. Aware of everything."

Fear tugged at me as I absorbed his words. "Are you saying she was planning an escape?"

"I'm saying I'm glad we didn't have to find out. I was concerned enough that I kept her under twenty-four-hour watch in a cell of her own."

I recalled what Mom had said about Matt's job and the inevitable worry that comes with caring for someone in law enforcement. "Your job sounds scary sometimes," I said, very sincerely.

"Most of the time it's not. Mostly it's a mix of routine and rewarding, with a dash of frustrating tossed in. But situations like this…."

"Situations like what?"

"I was in the Coast Guard before going into law enforcement. And we're not far from the Canadian border."

He was back to telling me without telling me. Was he trying to draw me out? Test me?

If so, could I blame him?

"Sorry, not following."

"I know how things can be sometimes. Jurisdictional overlap. Competing priorities. Agencies not sharing information."

"Is that what's going on here?"

"The Feds explained their interest in Amy by saying she has multiple warrants in multiple states under multiple aliases for check fraud, identity theft, burglary, and more."

"That doesn't surprise me."

"Here's the thing. Those guys don't bother with small stuff. No way they're driving up from Maryland for that."

"Maryland?"

"Their license plates. Two big SUVs. Eight big guys."

"Wow."

"For one petite woman."

No doubt about it: He definitely knew something was up. His presentation of the facts was more than suggestive — it was persuasive. If I hadn't already known what I already knew, I would have been all over this, eager to dive into the mystery.

"Okay," I said, "you convinced me. There's stuff here we don't know."

"Yep."

"And you're concerned about me nosing around more."

"Yep."

"And you know that normally, I'd be all over this."

"Yep."

"And you don't want that."

"Yep."

"Okay," I said. "Got it." I took a deep breath, then gave him what I hoped was my most reassuring expression. "So here's the thing, and please believe me when I say this: I've had more than my fill of mystery and danger."

Liar, my inner truth-teller said.

"For real?" he said.

"For real. My only focus now is bringing Emily's Eats back to life."

I couldn't tell if he believed me or not, but a smile came to his lips. "You're keeping the name?"

"Janie suggested it. In honor of my aunt, who meant so much to us both."

His focus on me intensified. "Sarah, I'm really glad you're staying in Eagle Cove."

"I'm glad, too," I said, pushing back a rush of feeling.

"We still haven't had that coffee."

"You're right, we haven't."

His eyes, direct and full of feeling, locked onto me, seeming to pull me in. "We need to do something about that."

"Guess you'll have to find a way to squeeze me into your busy schedule."

A gleam came. "Squeeze you in? I think I can manage that."

"In between all of your dates, of course," I said before I could stop myself.

A smile came to his lips. What I'd said amused him. "This town has the most energetic communications network on the planet."

"Is that so?"

"Though in this case, it isn't up-to-date."

My heart skipped a beat. "Oh?"

A smile played at the corner of his lips. "I'm not dating anyone right now."

"Even a certain real estate agent?"

"Her name is Cheryl. Very nice woman. We had dinner the other night. During which I told her she's not the woman for me."

He moved closer. I noticed he'd missed a spot shaving that morning — a patch of stubble on his strong jaw. I felt an urge to run my fingers over the roughness, suddenly finding it hard to breathe. I caught a hint of aftershave and a rush of unstoppable emotion roared through me.

"Matt," I whispered, completely unsure what I was about to say.

"Sarah," he said, not pulling away. "I...."

I heard it then — the roar of a high-performance sports car rounding the bend.

Matt heard it, too. He blinked and pulled back. A small gasp escaped my lips as the spell broke.

Claire's convertible zoomed into the driveway. As the engine rumbled, she lowered her sunglasses and gave us a knowing smile.

"Hey, Matt," she said.

"Hey, Claire," he said.

The two of them stared at each other. As much as they liked each other, they'd always been a bit competitive when it came to me.

Matt's gaze returned to me. "I should get going."

"Of course," I said.

"About that coffee," he added, his meaning perfectly clear. "I'm looking forward to it."

"Me, too," I said, far too truthfully.

He gave Claire a half-serious, half-playful look as he headed to his truck. "You two stay out of trouble, you hear?"

I wasn't able to keep my eyes off him as he climbed in and drove off.

When I turned to Claire, I found a knowing smile on her face.

"What?" I said, my cheeks flushing pink.

She patted her passenger seat.

"Hop in."

CHAPTER 31

I stared at my once-and-maybe-future best friend for a moment, wondering what she had planned for our afternoon. She looked so stylish in that snazzy red convertible, with her designer sunglasses and red lipstick, her blond hair tossed by the wind.

I had a million questions — the urge to know everything was nearly irresistible — but what was the point of asking?

With a deep breath, I climbed in.

Her knowing smile was still there. "Before we head out, anything you want to talk about?"

"No," I said firmly.

She snorted. "Uh huh."

My cheeks were like flaming bonfires now — oh, the burn! — but I decided to focus my attention on very carefully fastening my seatbelt.

After watching me settle in, Claire held out her hand, palm up. "Your phone, please."

I felt a jolt of excitement. "My phone?"

"Yes, please."

"Will I get it back?"

"Of course."

"You won't do one of those dramatic spy things where you smash it into a million bits so we can't be tracked or some such?"

"Sarah…."

I grabbed it from my purse and handed it over.

She powered it down and slipped it into her handbag. When her hand emerged, it held a black eye mask.

A thrill went through me. How mysterious. How *clandestine!*

She was enjoying this, I could tell.

As was I. The secrecy, intrigue, glamour — all of it.

I stared at the mask as she dropped it into my waiting hand. The fabric felt soft and thick. I knew exactly why she'd given it to me, but I still had to ask.

"Are you taking me to your secret spy lair?"

She nearly smiled but managed to stay solemn.

"At a secure undisclosed location?"

That almost got a laugh, but she was able to remain in character.

"Put it on and find out."

I slipped on the blindfold. The contours fit my face perfectly. Even if I tried, I wouldn't be able to see a thing.

"Matt suspects, by the way."

"I know," she said.

"And?"

"He's a big boy. He'll have to deal."

She pulled out. For the first few minutes, I tried keeping track of the turns and stops before giving up and settling in to enjoy the ride, admiring the speed and skill with which she took the twists and curves.

Neither of us spoke. With the convertible top down, the wind whipped over us, brisk and exhilarating, the engine's vibrations rumbling through me, the heated seat feeling wonderful against my back.

After about thirty minutes, the car slowed to a stop. I heard the sound of a gate opening. The convertible top closed over us. We drove forward slowly before descending via ramps down several levels. I guessed we were in a parking structure, perhaps even underground.

"Can I take this off?" I said.

"Sorry, not yet," she replied.

She brought the car to a stop, shut off the engine, grabbed her purse, and opened her door.

"How about now?"

"Patience."

She closed her door. I heard the click of boots on concrete. She opened my door and helped me out. The air was cool but still. Yes, we were definitely inside a structure of some sort. With her arm around my shoulder, she guided me about twenty yards. I heard the faint hum of machinery. A few seconds later, I heard a door open. We stepped into what I sensed was an elevator. The doors closed and we descended.

A few seconds later, the elevator stopped, the doors opened, and she led me out. The air was warmer than in the parking garage but still cool. I heard the murmur of nearby conversation. The place sounded like an office, but it smelled vaguely antiseptic. Kind of like....

A laboratory, perhaps?

Claire walked me down a corridor, her boot heels echoing on the hard floor and walls, then steered me into what I sensed was a room. I heard a door click shut.

"Before we go any further," she said, "I need you to understand that you cannot share any of this."

"What could I possibly share? I can't see a thing."

"I'm being serious," Claire said. "Very serious."

"Fine. I get it. My lips are zipped. This never happened. Any of it. Promise."

I heard her sigh. "Take off the blindfold."

I reached up and removed it, blinking as I adjusted to the light.

I was in what appeared to be a hospital room, small and windowless, modern and brightly lit. An array of equipment, blinking and beeping, surrounded a bed and chair.

The bed was occupied by a patient. An older woman, judging by the pale, wrinkled skin of the hand and arm resting on the blanket. A bandage covered part of her face. An IV was attached to her arm.

An instinct I didn't consciously understand gripped me and pulled me forward.

I stared at the woman on the bed and gasped.

Aunt Emily looked up at me, her gaze as direct and clear as ever.

"Sit down, Sarah," she said, her voice whispery but firm. "We have much to discuss."

THE END

MURDER SO COLD
EAGLE COVE MYSTERIES #2

When did muffins become so *deadly?!?*

I was expecting long hours and hard work when
I reopened my aunt's cafe in the heart of Eagle
Cove — but fishing an icy corpse from the lake
while delivering muffins?

Definitely not in my plans.

Now I'm getting dragged into danger — again
— and tangling with dark secrets I have no
business knowing.

Eagle Cove's handsome sheriff wants me safe
and on the sidelines. The mayor's convinced I'm
a murder magnet. My mom's terrified I might
get hurt — or worse.

But with a killer on the loose and so much at stake, I'm determined to protect those I love — even if doing so brings me to the end of my line....

MURDER SO PRETTY
EAGLE COVE MYSTERIES #3

Who knew flowers could be so *fatal?!?*

The annual Eagle Cove Flower Show is a huge deal in our little town, so when my cafe is hired to cater the opening reception, I'm determined to do everything I can to make the event a fun, festive, floral success.

All's going well until, amidst the revelry, I stumble upon the freshly murdered corpse of the head judge.

Now the town's in an uproar, media hordes are descending, and good friends are behaving very suspiciously.

With secrets swirling and loved ones in danger, I have no choice but to dig into this flowery, murdery mess —

Before the killer strikes again.

Who turned the barbeque into a *funeral pyre?!*

Eagle Cove's annual Fourth of July celebration is a cherished town tradition, filled with fireworks, fun, and favorite summer foods.

Then someone buries a body in the barbeque pit.

And with the lovely aroma of roasted pig comes an intriguing scent that folks can't quite put their finger on....

Murder So Tender is coming soon! To find out when, sign up for Nora's newsletter at AuthorNoraChase.com

Heartsprings Valley Romances
by Anne Chase

Christmas to the Rescue!
A Very Cookie Christmas
Sweet Apple Christmas
I Dream of Christmas
Chock Full of Christmas
The Christmas Sleuth

Eagle Cove Mysteries
by Nora Chase

Murder So Deep
Murder So Cold
Murder So Pretty
Murder So Tender

Emily Livingston Mysteries
by Nora Chase

A Death in Barcelona
From Rome, With Murder
Paris Is for Killers
In London We Die

Winter Tale series. In *Christmas to the Rescue!*, a young librarian named Becca gets caught in a blizzard on Christmas Eve, finds shelter with a handsome veterinarian named Nick, and ends up experiencing the most surprising, adventure-filled night of her life.

Nick and the Snowplow, told from Nick's point of view, shows what happens after Nick brings Becca home at the end of their whirlwind evening.

This story is available FOR FREE when you sign up for Anne Chase's email newsletter.

Go to AnneChase.com to sign up and get your free story.

ABOUT THE AUTHOR

As Anne Chase, I write small-town Christmas romances celebrating love during the most wonderful time of the year.

As Nora Chase, I write mysteries packed with murder, mayhem, and secrets galore.

My email newsletters are great ways to find out about my upcoming books.

Christmas romance: Sign up at AnneChase.com.

Mysteries: Sign up at AuthorNoraChase.com.

Thank you for being a reader.

Made in the USA
Monee, IL
27 June 2023

37819006R00184